WHAT TO DO WHEN THE MIND **TROUBLES** YOU

Also by Sirshree

Spiritual Masterpieces - Self Realisation books for serious seekers

The Secret of Awakening
100% Karma: Learn the Art of Conscious Karma that Liberates
100% Meditation: Dip into the Stillness of Pure Awareness
You are Meditation: Discover Peace and Bliss Within
Essence of Devotion: From Devotee to Divinity
Secrets of Shiva
The Supreme Quest: Your search for the Truth ends there where you are
The Greatest Freedom: Discover the key to an Awakened Living
Secret of The Third Side of The Coin
Seek Forgiveness & be Free: Liberation from Karmic Bondage
Passwords to a Happy Life: The Art of Being Happy in all Situations

Self Help Treasures - Self Development books for success seekers

The Source of Health: The Key to Perfect Health Discovery
Inner Ninety Hidden Infinity: How to build your book of values
Inner 90 for Youth: The secret of reaching and staying at the peak of success
The Source for Youth: You have the power to change your life
Inner Magic: The Power of self-talk
The Power of Present: Experience the Joy of the Now
You are Not Lazy: A story of shifting from Laziness to Success
Freedom From Fear, Worry, Anger: How to be cool, calm and courageous
The Little Gita of Problem Solving: Gift of 18 Solutions to Any Problem
Discover Your Real Wealth: If Money is the Means, Then What is the End?

New Age Nuggets - Practical books on applied spirituality and self help

The Source: Power of Happy Thoughts
Secret of Happiness: Instant Happiness - Here and Now!
Help God to Help You: Whatever you do, do it with a smile
Ultimate Purpose of Success: Achieving Success in all five aspects of life
Celebrating Relationships: Bringing Love, Life, Laughter in Your Relations
Everything is a Game of Beliefs: Understanding is the Whole Thing
Detachment From Attachment: Gift of Freedom From Suffering
Emotional Freedom Through Spiritual Wisdom

Profound Parables - Fiction books containing profound truths

Beyond Life: Conversations on Life After Death
The One Above: What if God was your neighbour?
The Warrior's Mirror: The Path To Peace
Master of Siddhartha: Revealing the Truth of Life and After-life
Put Stress to Rest: Utilizing Stress to Make Progress
The Source @ Work: A Story of Inspiration from Jeeodee

SIRSHREE

Author of the bestseller *The Source*

WHAT TO DO
WHEN THE MIND
TROUBLES
YOU

Encountering the Mind Instead of Escaping it

What To Do When The Mind Troubles You
Encountering the Mind Instead of Escaping it
By **Sirshree** Tejparkhi

Copyright © Tejgyan Global Foundation
All Rights Reserved 2019

Tejgyan Global Foundation is a charitable organization
with its headquarters in Pune, India.

ISBN : 978-81-943200-5-0

Published by WOW Publishings Pvt. Ltd., India

First edition published in December 2019

Copyrights are reserved with Tejgyan Global Foundation and publishing rights are vested exclusively with WOW Publishings Pvt. Ltd. This book is sold subject to the condition that it shall not by way of trade or otherwise, be lent, resold, hired out, or otherwise circulated without the publisher's prior written consent in any form of binding or cover other than that in which it is published and without a similar condition including this condition being imposed on the subsequent purchaser and without limiting the rights under copyright reserved above, no part of this publication may be reproduced, stored in or introduced into a retrieval system, or transmitted, in any form, or by any means, electronic, mechanical, photocopying, recording or otherwise, without the prior written permission of both the copyright owner and the above-mentioned publisher of this book. Any person who does any unauthorized act in relation to this publication may be liable to criminal prosecution and civil claims for damages.

Although the author and publisher have made every effort to ensure accuracy of content in this book, they hereby disclaim any liability to any party for any loss, damage, or disruption caused by errors or omissions, resulting from negligence, accident, or any other cause. Readers are advised to take full responsibility to exercise discretion in understanding and applying the content of this book.

*To the great souls
who attained mastery over the mind
and bestowed the gift of their wisdom
for the generations to come.*

Table Of Contents

Preface		9
PART 1 – Understanding The Troubled Mind		**13**
1.	Fly It and Realize Your Destiny	15
2.	Retain the Purity of Awareness	21
3.	The Opportunity with the Troubled Mind	25
4.	Dealing with Emotions	29
5.	Secret of Happiness	35
6.	The Problem Underlying All Problems	41
7.	Essence of Thoughts, Gravity of Intent	45
8.	Sow the Right Seeds of Emotions	51
9.	Change the Momentum of Your Thoughts	57
10.	Reflect on Yourself	63

PART 2 – Encountering The Troubled Mind   69

11. Magic of Self-Talk   71
12. Reframe Your Self-Talk   75
13. Magic of Acceptance   83
14. Modalities for Acceptance   89
15. Bother Then, When Then Becomes Now   95
16. Learn by Hindsight to Relax with Foresight   101
17. No One to be Blamed   105
18. Hold Onto Your Happy Hat   111
19. Drop The Copycat Habit   115
20. Consciously Create Your Future   119
      Appendix   124

Preface

Imagine a scene where you are walking on a swaying rope, carrying a bomb in your hands. Because of the bomb, you feel paranoid and overwhelmed with all kinds of emotions. You get irritated; you fume at others; at times, you get scared; you feel dejected.

You feel like throwing the bomb away, but then it boomerangs back on you. Thus, you feel helpless holding it in your custody. Neither can you escape it by throwing it away, nor can you carry it along.

What can you do in this situation?

You may find yourself clueless about the answer and wonder whether there can be a solution to this. But it is the truth that we all are carrying a bomb with us – our very own mind it is!

The mind is always with us. There's not a moment when it is non-existent, except when we are asleep, and even then, it asserts its presence through dreams. From morning till night, we carry it with us. At times, it's like a monkey that keeps jumping from one topic to another without affording you any relaxation. At other times, it's like a wild elephant that doesn't pay heed to you and runs amok, causing you pain and regret. At times, it is like a serpent that pulls you down, filling you with the poison of hatred, resentment and ill-will.

You have to reach your destination with this bomb. You hear that great masters, who have walked this earth, have attained mastery over it and achieved feats that no one else has. You would also wish to attain such prowess. But when you see your mind get the better of you in various situations, you feel defeated and hopeless.

In everyday situations, if we favor the mind and give in to its whims and fancies, it behaves well, only for a short while though. However, the moment, we go against its desires, it torments us. You see that appeasing the mind and maintaining your composure becomes a tedious task, attaining the supreme state of those masters is farfetched. Hence, you try to satisfy the whims of the mind, only to find yourself vacillating in the dualities of shortlived pleasure and perpetual sorrow.

Most people find it overwhelming and uncomfortable to confront their troubled minds and hence try to escape it by finding temporary solace in distractions, vices and entertainment. They engage in sensory pleasures like watching TV, surfing the net, binge-watching, being glued to mobile screens, worry-eating, worry-shopping. However, this doesn't solve their underlying issues that keep re-surfacing.

Given all this, we begin to believe that attaining the supreme state of ultimate freedom is possible only for the chosen fortunate ones; that we are the unfortunate ones.

But what if you were told that the mind can be trained and can become your best asset in leading you on your path towards the supreme goal of life?

This book shows you how. Replete with several techniques and examples, it helps you gain control over your mind well before it slips into the spiral of negative thinking, which makes you dwell in the quicksand of gloom, despair, resentment, frustration, anxiety and stress. The methods and understanding provided in this book can help you emerge a winner, instead of sinking into depression.

As you master these techniques, you will see yourself brimming with positive energy. Your latent potential will be unleashed. You can explore your infinite possibilities. Your life will be filled with happiness, wonder, peace and love. You will live in gratitude that you could experience such a miraculous life with the very same mind that was tormenting you.

Do you find this too good to be true? Not after you have read the chapters that follow…

If you are willing to open the door of possibilities to a supreme life, then this book is for you.

This book shows you how to deal with the troubled mind using a two-pronged approach:

- Coming to terms with the troubled state of mind and restoring its positive healthy state.
- Delving deep into the fire of the troubled mind to understand your emotions, introspect your thoughts and their underlying beliefs.

This book provides insights into effective ways of dealing with the troubled mind, well before the onset of depression. By practicing the techniques explained in this book, you can pull the mind out of the doldrums of despair and re-establish the natural state of peace, poise and joy.

The book is divided into two parts:

Part 1 – Understanding the Troubled Mind, explains how the troubled mind behaves and provides insights on how we can change our perspective to counter the antics of the mind.

Part 2 – Encountering the Troubled Mind, outlines powerful techniques to encounter your mind and shift from the abyss of negativity to the heights of positivity.

Written in a simple lucid language with various examples, this book provides tips of practical spirituality that can be applied in everyday life situation.

It is recommended that you read the book from beginning to end, so as to derive its full benefit.

By understanding and practically applying what's outlined in the chapters that follow, you will emerge a winner by encountering your mind instead of escaping it. You will dwell in love, bliss and peace which is your birthright.

PART 1

UNDERSTANDING THE **TROUBLED** MIND

1
Fly It and Realize Your Destiny

A small airplane landed on an agricultural field. The pilot went his way, abandoning the aircraft, and never returned.

When a farmer, who was ploughing the field, saw the airplane, he wondered, "What is this strange thing?" He had never seen an airplane before. He thought for a while and then tied two bullocks to the airplane. Now, it became his bullock cart. He began to till the land. Let's consider the name of this farmer to be 'A'.

Farmer 'A' later sold his land to Farmer 'B' along with his bullock cart. Thus, he ended up selling the airplane to Farmer 'B' for the price of a bullock cart.

Now, what did Farmer 'B' do with it?

Farmer 'B' mulled over it and speculated that it could be a machine that could run on its own without the bullocks. He tinkered with it and it suddenly came to life. Now, the airplane became a tractor! Farmer 'B' used it productively to plough his fields.

One day, a wise monk happened to pass by. He saw Farmer 'B' using the airplane as a tractor. He thundered, "Fly it!

Fly it and realize your destiny!" But Farmer 'B' failed to understand the message. He sold the airplane-turned-tractor to Farmer 'C' at the price of a tractor.

The son of Farmer 'C' returned home having completed his education. He watched the tractor and figured out, "This thing can fly!" He did some research, gathered information and got the plane flying.

Farmer 'C' began to earn a lot. He too eventually sold the land, but not the plane. Wherever he went, he flew the plane.

So, what's the point?

Believe it or not, you too have got a wonderful airplane! No, you don't need to look around; it's your very own body-mind mechanism. It's like an airplane. But due to lack of knowledge and expertise many of us use it like a bullock cart or a tractor. Very few are able to use it as an airplane.

Contemplate for a minute on how you use your body-mind mechanism.

Till date, perhaps you may not have used it to its fullest potential. The body and mind could be lethargic or hyperactive. The mind could be moody, complaining and rigid. And when the mind keeps vacillating according to its moods and whims, you may trust whatever it says.

When your mind grumbles, "No one cares for me… I am getting bored… People are selfish…," you become upset. When your mind says, "I am tired… It's impossible to accomplish this task… I can't do it…," you give up.

If your mind declares an entertainment break and sprawls on the sofa, holding the TV remote, you happily agree to it. This means you are driven by the fancies of your mind.

When the mind reigns over our discretion, it becomes dominant. Emotional upheavals can take their toll on our vitality. The most trivial undesirable event or an inability to reason with people can cause us anxiety and disappointment. If one is not sensitive to this growing tendency of the mind to dwell on negative emotions, one could possibly slip into depression.

Depression sets in when the thinking machine loses direction. But the key thing to note is that we are not just thinking machines. Rather the thinking machine is an instrument that we use. Careful observation will show that we are not our bodies, since we can observe our bodies. Whatever is being observed is not the observer. Even our thoughts can be observed. We can take some time out to observe our thoughts as they arise and subside. As we practice this, we find that we are not our thoughts too. We are the knower of our thoughts, the knower of our mind. This knowing continues to exist even in the gap between two thoughts.

This deep knowing or consciousness is the essence of life. It is the Source of life. Everything arises from this Source. It is who-we-truly-are, beyond our body and mind. Consciousness can be experienced as the feeling of being alive, of being awake to whatever is happening. This song of "Being alive" is being played constantly; we are that song. Being aware of this song gives the experience of pure joy, unconditional and boundless, independent of the world, untouched by situations.

However, just as we cannot view ourselves clearly through a mirror that is decorated with all sorts of designs, who-we-truly-are cannot experience itself and express its potential to the fullest if the body-mind is tainted with the impurities of wrong beliefs and tendencies.

Such a body-mind can pose hurdles in our path. We cannot make progress with such a body-mind.

> It's like a bird that is trapped in a cage. The bird keeps complaining about the leaking roof of the cage. But even if the bird were set free, it would hover around the cage and ponder about repairing its roof. It could have, otherwise, flown high in the vast sky. It could have explored its infinite

hidden possibilities. But it is not used to such freedom. Hence, it's thinking is limited to the problems within the cage.

Just like this bird, we tend to identify ourselves with our body and mind and consider the problems of the body and mind to be ours. It is essential to experientially know who-we-truly-are and be detached from our body-mind. Also, the body-mind needs to be trained in such a way that it becomes instrumental for our best expression.

> When we buy a new mobile phone, we explore its features so that we can use its features to our benefit. If we use its basic features, then we are not making its best use.

Similarly, our body, mind and intellect have immense latent powers. Unless we use them to our benefit, we won't realize our body-mind's highest potential. We will end up using it like a bullock-cart all our life just like Farmer 'A' did.

God doesn't play favorites. He bestows the seed of highest potential within each one of us. It's up to each of us how we train our body and mind to unleash our inherent potential. We experience true contentment only when we realize who we truly are and express our divine qualities in all situations of life.

Such a body-mind can then create wonders like what has been created by great saints like Lord Buddha, Jesus, Lord Mahavira, Saint Dnyaneshwar, Guru Nanak, to name a few. The Buddha attained mastery over sorrow and reached the state of perfection where the mind is rooted in heightened awareness, peace and bliss, regardless of external situations.

All the incredible scientific discoveries and inventions could become possible only because of the trained body-minds of scientists. Till today, many generations have reaped the benefits of their perseverance and will continue to do so hereafter. The same possibility, as these saints and scientists, lies within each of us.

In the forthcoming chapters, we will learn about how to update and upgrade our mind. Then our body-mind will not just become an airplane, but can also fly like a rocket. As the wise monk said, "You can fly it and realize your destiny!" In other words, it can not only cope with and overcome challenging situations but also unleash your hidden potential.

But before that, we will learn about who we truly are. The understanding of who-we-truly-are is an essential prerequisite to upgrade our mind. We will consider this in the next chapter.

Action plan

- Contemplate on what kind of body-mind you have received along with its strengths and weaknesses.

2
Retain the Purity of Awareness

Imagine that you are in a garden with a camera, shooting a video of beautiful flowers. You wish to capture the complete view of the garden, replete with all its details, including the greenery, flowers, birds etc.

You zoom in on a lovely marigold flower in full bloom and are about to capture its beauty in your camera, when you spot a honey bee hovering over it. You're overjoyed at the entire scene and wish to capture it all.

But lo! The bee flies over and perches on your camera lens. What you see now through the camera is a black blotch that blocks the view through your camera viewfinder. Try as you may, the bee doesn't budge. Now you wish that the bee would leave the lens and return to the flower, so that you can capture a complete and clear picture!

While this is a common occurrence with photographers, this example has a profound implication when it comes to understanding how the mind brews trouble and how we get entangled in its exploits.

We are here to derive joy from the experience of the world, replete with all its happenings. But, while we are intent on capturing the experience of the world in the invisible camera of our awareness, we struggle at it. Why?

Because the incidents that occur in our lives are like the flowers in the garden. They attract the honey bees of thoughts and emotions. Yes! Incidents and thoughts occur together as part of the same scene, triggering associated emotions.

But then, we allow the thoughts and emotions that occur along with incidents to pervade our awareness. As a result, we cannot witness the incident as-it-is. Our witnessing becomes corrupted by the thoughts that shade our perception. The lens of awareness gets sullied by emotions that cling on, denying us a pure view of the incidents or situations in our life.

The truth is that an incident or situation, in and by itself, is neither happy nor sad. It is the thoughts that occur in the situation that stick onto us, which shade them as happy or sad.

> You are waiting for your friend to join you to attend an important meeting. Your friend has not turned up. As time passes, you start cursing her, "She is always late. Why can't she come on time? I have commitments to keep. Next time, I will go on my own… and so on." By the time your friend turns up, you are fuming with anger.

The moment an incident occurs, thoughts arise along with it. However, you separate the incident from its accompanying thoughts. You mistakenly consider the incident as something "outside" you and the thoughts as a part of you. This allows them to intrude and pollute your awareness. The more you entertain such thoughts, the more are the ripples created in your pure awareness. It triggers emotions in your body. You start feeling anger and frustration within you.

What can we do to regain our original purity of awareness?

Just as the photographer sends back the bee from the lens over to the flowers, similarly, we need to learn the knack of distancing ourselves from our thoughts and emotions, viewing them as a part of the incident itself.

We may even use a gesture of waving our hands before our eyes, as if we are wiping the screen of awareness, clean. This gesture serves as an anchor for us to distance ourselves from the thoughts that have invaded our awareness. By doing so, we retain the purity of our awareness; we maintain the clarity of our perception.

Then no thought can trouble us; no emotion can weigh us down. In other words, we can then distance ourselves from our own minds and observe, so that we remain untouched by the vagaries of our thoughts.

Let's practice a meditation to understand this. First read the instruction and then practice the meditation.

1. Before beginning, you may set a timer for five to ten minutes. You may use your cell phone, a computer, a clock or a watch for that.

2. Sit in a comfortable posture and close your eyes.

3. Observe every thought that arises within. Tell every thought that arises, "You have intruded into my awareness. Go back to where you belong – on the other side with the situation. I will see you just as a thought, nothing more."

4. Don't borrow the story that the thought presents. Persist with this approach towards every thoughts that arises, no matter what the thought may say.

5. A thought may arise, "What's the use of doing this?" or "This exercise is futile," or "How much time is remaining, I hope the timer hasn't stopped."

6. Send every thought over to where it belongs – the world – and mentally say "Next…".

7. When the timer goes off, open your eyes and reflect on any shift in perspective that you may have gained.

While shifting to pure awareness is indeed possible for all, some may find it easier to weed out thoughts from their awareness and view them with detachment. Others may find it difficult to do so, especially when situations are challenging. Thoughts tend to cling onto awareness so tightly that we lose ourselves in the content of the thoughts. For instance, if the thought that occurs in an incident says, "There's no hope," or "People cannot be trusted", we get attached to the story that the thought conveys and treat it as "my" story. We experience all sorts of negative feelings like hopelessness, distrust and sadness.

In situations when thoughts cling onto awareness, it becomes difficult to distance ourselves from those thoughts. We get completely drawn into those thoughts and get identified with the story. We believe that whatever happens with the character in the story is happening with us. We are overwhelmed by all sorts of negative emotions.

In the next chapter, we will look at how negative emotions can be considered as an opportunity for growth and raising our awareness.

Action plan

- In situations where you feel overwhelmed by negative thoughts and emotions, practice the meditation explained earlier.

3
The Opportunity with the Troubled Mind

Consider a hypothetical case of a person, who is in a particular type of coma. There are two injections available to treat his condition and bring him out of coma. You need to choose one of them.

With the first injection, he will emerge from his coma and lead a common man's life. Of course, he will fulfil all his worldly duties. You will see him performing all routine activities; he will sit, eat, chat and go around. He will watch TV, attend parties. He will be busy with some activity or the other. And when his time comes, he will pass away.

Thus, the first injection gives him a routine mechanical life, where he sleepwalks through a mundane repetitive existence without exploring any of his hidden possibilities. He has shut down his sensitivity to the world of subtle feelings and hence, never gets to learn about the value of compassion, empathy, patience, courage or resilience during his uneventful life.

On the other hand, with the second injection, he can open up to a life of infinite possibilities. However, he also runs the risk of experiencing intermittent bouts of sadness, anxiety, stress and gloominess. There is also a 60% risk of him committing suicide. At the same time, there is a 40% possibility that he will create something invaluable, which can bring about a transformation in the world.

As a result of the second injection, it is certain that he will suffer bouts of despondency. He will be exposed to overwhelming emotions that can even derail him at times. But there is also the likelihood that he will rise above the highs and lows of life and discover the supreme state of awareness – the birthright of all humans.

You have to make a choice. Which injection will you administer? Contemplate on this for a few minutes.

Now, place yourself in his shoes and contemplate your choice.

If you are leading a mechanical life, reacting to situations without paying heed to what's brewing within you, adopting a hardened and insensitive approach to whatever you feel, then the first injection has already been administered and is working in your life!

If you wish to lead a novel life, open to immense possibilities of growth and higher expression, of course with the risk of intermittent bouts of distress, then it's time for you to take the second injection. It will help you fulfil the very purpose of your life. You will lead your life by being who-you-truly-are, as pure awareness beyond the vagaries of your mind and body.

What does it mean to take the second injection?

The "second injection" symbolizes the higher choice to risk feeling negative emotions so as to grow beyond them. Taking the second injection implies looking at the occurrence of sadness and distress with a positive perspective. Don't consider it as failure or a lowly state. When you feel sad, gloomy, dispirited or upset, remember to thank yourself that you are not in coma.

Congratulate yourself that you are probably on the verge of a breakthrough in your journey of growth, that in turn can help others around you. The negative emotions are just a side-effect in the process of growth. It helps to encounter these emotions with an attitude of gratitude that they are teaching you valuable lessons of life, helping you grow and mature.

The occurrence of these bouts of negative emotions is actually a reminder of your strength and not weakness. It has come to unleash your latent potential and push you towards your higher purpose. If you are convinced about this, then you can gracefully tide through these emotions instead of turning away from them.

When we consider sadness and distress as our failure, it will keep increasing. Feeling sad, anxious or despondent is a by-product of a higher choice that we have made and now it is our duty to honor and fulfil that choice. We cannot put the higher purpose behind this choice at stake by stopping in between because of the negative emotions that it triggers.

However, if you forget this and blame others for your state, then it only sets the stage for further recurrences. As long as you consider others as a cause of your happiness or sorrow, you will depend upon them. You will feel depressed when people ignore you, disregard you. You will be pleased when they appreciate you and treat you with respect. The momentary pleasure that you derive from the desirable behavior of others will make you temporarily feel that you have come out of your distress because of their behavior. But in reality, they have only helped you connect with your own true nature – pure awareness. That's why you feel happy.

People and incidents are mere pretexts to connect with our true nature. If we understand this, we will become free in a true sense. The blame game that was going on due to lack of awareness will be over. We will not bother much about how other people behave. We will always remain happy and overcome the 60% risk of sadness, grief and anxiety.

Let's understand it with the example of a caterpillar. A caterpillar strives to come out of its cocoon. It applies pressure, which in turn strengthens its wings. Soon, it emerges as a beautiful butterfly. If it doesn't apply pressure, it remains stuck inside the cocoon.

Similarly, when you go through uncomfortable feelings, understand that they have arisen to release your potential. Thus, when you tide through negative emotions, tell yourself that God is safeguarding you; this is part of transforming from a caterpillar to a beautiful butterfly. Your mind will then become quiet.

When you choose the second injection, your level of awareness will gradually rise. You will understand that the bouts of negative emotions are temporary and that they will pass. You will also gain clarity that all negative emotions are experienced at the level of your physical body and not by who-you-truly-are.

If we are able to fully immerse ourselves in the experience of what is being felt by the body-mind and feel it fully, we can regain our purity of awareness; we can resume functioning from our true nature of pure awareness. Let's understand this in the next chapter.

Action Plan

- Observe the negative emotions experienced by your body. Tell yourself, "These emotions are with my body-mind, not with the one who I really am."

4
Dealing with Emotions

Rima organized a training program for her team. She sent them an invite for the program but no one accepted her request. Now, Rima was in two minds – whether to go ahead with it or cancel. She was angry that no one cared to respond to her.

Most of us feel angry in such situations. We also go through other feelings like boredom, confusion, depression, envy, fear, guilt, hatred. These feelings reflect on our body in the form of physical symptoms called emotions. These symptoms are nothing but the subconscious mind's reaction to the thought that triggered that feeling. Unaware of the nuances of dealing with emotions, we are uncomfortable of facing them.

In the above example, Rima experienced the uncomfortable feeling of anger at her team's disregard. Likewise, we experience different feelings when we are alone or with people. Let's understand them with some more examples.

    a) Mita finished her exams and returned home. The last few weeks were very hectic for her. She was fully immersed in her studies. Now that the exams were over, she was left with nothing to do; she suddenly started feeling a void within her. She felt the urge to do something to get rid of that feeling. She switched on the TV. Not sure of what to watch, she kept toggling between TV channels. Nothing interested her. After some time she opened the fridge to grab some chocolates. Then she scrolled through her WhatsApp messages for some time and chatted with her friends. This is boredom.

b) Amar skipped his classes and spent the day binge-watching a TV series at his friend's house. When he returned home, he was scared of what his parents would say. His heart was beating at a faster pace. His hands were trembling with fear.

We can see that an uncomfortable feeling not only comes from external stimuli, but also arises from within us as a result of change in mood, a sudden recall of some memory, or change in surroundings. We experience feelings as emotions in our body. As these emotions seem uncomfortable, we immediately try to get rid of them.

Most people don't know how to handle their emotions. Whenever they face an uncomfortable feeling, they either explode or suppress it within. When they spew it out on others, it results in anger, hatred and envy, thereby creating a tendency in them for repeat occurrences. Blurting out emotions also has a disparaging effect on relationships. Thus, they may temporarily safeguard their physical health by expressing anger or resentment on others, but it is at the cost of harmony in their relations. Ultimately it leads them to regret.

Conversely, when they suppress the emotion within, they may appear calm outside, but may simmer within. If they continue to suppress it for a long time, it eventually becomes unbearable, causing them to explode like a volcano. When emotions are suppressed for long, they also lead to various kinds of illnesses. Studies have shown that such suppressed emotions affect various parts of the body. For example, fear can affect the kidneys and the urinary bladder, hatred can affect the lungs, guilt can affect the neck, depression can affect the feet, too much of emotional burden can cause shoulder pain.

When we suppress or express our emotions, it sets the stage for future recurrence of these emotions. Thus, these ways of dealing with emotions only provide temporary relief. They are escape mechanisms that we have been conditioned to use as we don't know any better way of handling our emotions.

For a permanent way of dealing with emotions, there is a third way. Witness the emotions from a detached standpoint. Detached witnessing consists of three aspects:

1. **Understanding** – When emotions overpower you, you get identified with them. You feel as if they are happening *with* you. Hence, in order to witness them separately, you need to first detach from them. You can do so by consciously asking yourself, "Exactly what is happening to whom?" In short: **Exactly what to whom?**

For instance, if an emotion of anger has arisen, what exactly is happening? You will see that your breath has become rapid and shallow. Your ears have become warm. Your heart is beating more rapidly. You feel a pressure in your forehead or in the chest. You feel sudden tension in your arms, neck or shoulders. Instead of being swayed by the story around which your anger is based, focus on these sensations. Observe them for what they truly are.

The next aspect is *to whom* it is happening. You find that the emotions are felt in your body and your mind has declared that, "I am angry." But who-you-truly-are is separate from the body and the mind. You can stand apart and be aware of what is happening with your mind. You are the knower of what is happening. It is not happening *to* you. You are pure awareness with the ripples of anger arising within its field. You need to distance yourself from these ripples to retain the purity of your awareness. The more we get to actually witness this in situations, the easier it becomes to detach from emotions.

The next truth that becomes evident when we witness is that every emotion arises, plays out for some time and then subsides. Thus, it is temporary, just like a wave in the ocean. It will arise and then subside. If you witness it, you will become free from it. The next time when the emotion arises, its severity will be lower than before. Thus, as you watch it from a detached standpoint with this understanding, gradually its effect diminishes. Soon, you will find that you are able to maintain poise in the same situations where you used to get troubled earlier. Thus, this approach involves confronting the mind, encountering the emotions.

As you witness the feeling of fear from a detached standpoint, all your residual fears also get uprooted along with this emotion and slowly you emerge as a courageous winner. If you have hatred against someone and you witness this emotion from a detached standpoint; compassion will automatically arise within you.

However, when we lack the right understanding, the mind will try to do away with the feeling by escaping and instigating you to indulge in shopping, chatting, browsing, eating something, etc. It either escapes by distracting attention or by reacting in the situation. With this, you may feel relieved and relaxed, but it's temporary. After some period, you will again have the same feeling. Hence instead of escaping, witness your emotions with the right understanding and soon you will be free from them.

2. **Equanimity** – The other aspect of detached witnessing is equanimity. We feel aversion for painful sensations and crave for pleasurable sensations. Equanimity is all about seeing painful and pleasurable emotions alike without aversion or craving. When you see things with equanimity, you experience a sense of evenness where there is neither a "like" nor "dislike" for what is being witnessed.

In case of feelings such as anger, depression, or resentment, our brain invariably misinterprets the situation and ascribes an exaggerated weight to them. As a result, the emotion feels heavy and intense. When we slow down the mind and watch the emotion with an attitude of equanimity, we are able to question the weight of the emotion. What may appear to be a heavyweight emotion of the order of say 50 kg, will then turn out to be not even 5 grams! Such clarity can arise from deep observation with equanimity.

3. **Alertness** – It is essential to be vigilant to remain detached. When we are not vigilant, the natural tendency is to identify with the emotion and create further stories about it. We need to have an alert awareness that is focused on itself. We need to vigilantly use

emotions as hooks to shift our focus on who-we-truly-are, on pure awareness.

Using these three aspects, when you witness emotions from a detached standpoint, you feel them fully; you encounter them completely. This helps provide a new input to your brain and to your subconscious mind in turn when the same emotion arises next time. You will be able to maintain your calm in situations where you used to get angry. You will not get troubled by the same problems as much. You will choose to respond to problems creatively instead of reacting to them, thus making the same problems stepping stones for your progress. You will no longer escape from situations.

Let's practice a meditation to witness your emotions from a detached standpoint. First read the instructions and then practice the meditation.

1. Before beginning, you may set a timer for ten to fifteen minutes. You may use your cell phone, a computer, a clock or a watch for that.

2. Close your eyes. With the detachment of a spectator, watch which emotions are present in which part of your body—above your stomach, on the sides, in the chest, on the back, or elsewhere.

3. Whatever be the situation, watch it only as an observer. Do not keep any attachment to any emotion. Do not try to change anything.

4. Wherever you experience emotions on your body, focus there, and check how it feels – heavy or light, pleasant or unpleasant, joyful or fearful, worrisome or anxious. Simply experience these emotions, without labeling them as good or bad.

5. Go through your whole body, part by part. During this inner journey, you will realize that no emotion is permanent. If it's there one moment, the next moment it's not. If it's there today, tomorrow it's not. Just observe as a silent spectator.

6. Without being affected by the events taking place outside or within, experience the emotions.

7. When the timer goes off, slowly open your eyes. Remain in this state for some time and then proceed with your usual activities.

We have seen how we can effectively deal with emotions in order to distance them and retain the purity of awareness. When we practice this meditation in silence every day, we will be able to learn and master it.

In the next chapter, we will look at the connection betweeen the desires of the mind and our quest for happiness.

Action Plan

- In your daily life situations, observe the various emotions that you go through when you are alone and also with people. Notice when you try to divert your attention to avoid discomfort. Identify the escape mechanisms that you've unconsciously been using. Maintain a written log of these instances.

5
Secret of Happiness

A person found his cat to be too much of a nuisance. In order to get rid of it, he repeatedly tried carrying it to faraway places to be abandoned. Each time, however, the cat would somehow find its way back home. Despite his best attempts, he failed in his objective.

One day, he happened to recount one such incident to his friend. "I took the cat deep into the jungle one day and left it there," he said, "but in the process, I myself got lost and could not find my way home!" "Oh! Then how did you return?" asked the friend. The man smiled, "I simply followed the cat, and it brought me home!"

The very cat the person wanted to be rid of served to lead him home when he was woefully lost. Similarly, the very mind due to which we feel flustered and dejected can become a vehicle for attaining a life of freedom, joy and peace and also radiate it to others. It can become a tool for our salvation. If the mind is going to be so helpful, then we need to understand it deeply.

The mind has been described using several metaphors. It has been called a monkey – always jumping about and indulging in acrobatics. It has also been described as a cat – one that slinks into a house to quietly have milk and then disappears, one that sometimes carries dead rats into the house and one that often becomes an impediment during religious rituals – being a perennial cause of distraction.

Situations change from time to time. In these situations, things may happen as per the mind's will or otherwise. When things happen as the mind wishes, it makes us happy. Otherwise, it troubles us. We get angry when there is delay in the fulfilment of the mind's wishes. When things don't turn up exactly as the mind wishes, we experience sorrow. Thus, our state of mind changes from time to time based on the fulfilment of our desires.

The wandering mind harbors desires that are insatiable. Whenever we acquire whatever we desire, the restlessness of the mind caused by that desire subsides temporarily. This allows us to experience the happiness that always exists within us, but only for a short while.

We don't realize that the happiness that we experienced was always present within us. Hence, we wrongly connect the happiness with the objects of our desire. The more we experience such momentary happiness, the more convinced we are that we can get happiness from people, objects and circumstances. Hence, we continue to desire those things. This comes at the cost of losing the real source of happiness that is always available within us!

Since the experience of happiness is momentary, we entertain some other desire as soon as the earlier one is fulfilled. Thus, we get caught up in this vicious cycle of desires. If we try to control our desires, the mind rebels. We fall victim to the idiosyncrasies of the mind and remain in the duality of joy and sorrow at the mercy of the mind.

So, what's the point?

Desire, in itself, is never the cause of sorrow, happiness or anger. Sorrow arises due to the habit of chasing our desires, based on the belief that we can be happy only when they are fulfilled. The habit of desiring veils our ever-present blissful nature.

While satisfying desires, our mind tries to weigh and assess everything on its own terms. The mind thinks, "If I accomplish a certain task, then I will be happy… If people praise me for my success, then I will be happy… If no one pays attention to me, I will feel unhappy… If I am belittled in front of others, I will be angry… If I don't have enough bank balance, I will be unhappy."

Due to this habit of the mind, it postpones happiness by attaching preconditions; it keeps waiting to be happy. Whenever you feel dissatisfied or unfulfilled, whenever you sense that you are not happy, be sure that the mind is postponing happiness based on fulfilment of its imaginary preconditions. Happiness can never be experienced if it is subject to fulfilling such conditions. True happiness is unconditional.

When we try to reason and conceptualize happiness, we indulge in thinking. This takes us far away from our inherent joyful nature. We seek imaginary happiness in the content of our thoughts.

The mind is inherently extroverted in nature. It always thinks about the objects and people in the external world with the underlying desire to derive unobstructed happiness from them. However, nothing, no one can ever make us perfectly happy.

Seeking happiness in the world is like chasing one's own shadow endlessly. Like the shadow, happiness always eludes us. We experience sorrow and dissatisfaction when we move away from pure happiness which is our true nature.

The pleasure that we derive from the world is short-lived, and hence we continue to seek more happiness restlessly. We continue to waste our precious creative energy in this endeavor. We believe that's the way of life because we see everyone else around us doing the same. But it's like chasing the horizon. Desires will be fulfilled, but they won't give us true lasting happiness.

The happiness that the mind seeks can never be experienced. Happiness does not lie in thoughts or the content of thoughts. True happiness can only be experienced in the stillness beyond the mind. There can never be "peace of mind", since the mind itself is noise.

True peace and happiness are always available in what lies beyond the mind.

Happiness can only be experienced in the present, not in the bygone past or the imagined future. The present is the only reality that can be experienced; and it is always available to us! And this, in itself, is the cause for celebration. However, the present slips away in the constant stream of thoughts. We chase after shadows by pursuing our notions about happiness.

Hence, instead of getting distracted in the topics of the external world, we can use the same mind to return to our blissful state of being. Lend the right direction to the mind to turn inward and the wandering mind becomes focused and exceptionally creative. We can feel surprised about how the very situation that was giving us sorrow can then give us happiness. Making the mind instrumental for knowing our true nature is the ultimate use of the mind.

By giving in to the ways of the mind or by giving up, we can't attain freedom from the mind. We are never certain of being happy forever. Instead, by employing the mind at our service just like the person put the cat to service in the earlier example, we can attain lasting happiness. In a true sense, we become its master.

Let's experience the state of freedom from desires with the practice of meditation.

Read through the instructions first and then practice this meditation.

1. Before beginning, you may set a timer for ten minutes. You may use your cell phone, a computer, a clock or a watch for that.

2. Sit in a comfortable posture and close your eyes.

3. Ask yourself, "What are the desires occupying my mind now?"

4. Observe the various desires that arise. Several desires may arise. "No one should disturb me", "Let me eat some food", "Let me open my eyes", "Let me see what others are doing."

5. Just witness them. Tell yourself, "I am free from all desires. Neither do I desire that something should happen, nor do I desire that it should not happen. I am free from all desires."

6. There is a possibility of having a desire, "I have been sitting for so long. Let me stand for some time." Even if any such a desire occurs, don't act upon it.

7. Train your mind in such a way that you will be able to easily proclaim, "Now, I can sit here without getting up at all, because I am now free from all desires."

8. When you completely accept the situation, then a desire may arise, "Let this meditation continue forever." Then also tell yourself, "It is fine even if the meditation doesn't continue. I am free from that desire too."

    When you are able to proclaim in this way, how will your state be!? How is the state of freedom from all desires? Try to experience that state at least for some time. Experience this freedom at least for some time.

9. When the timer goes off, open your eyes.

Having gained a new perspective about desires, let's understand how to look at problems in the next chapter.

Action plan

- Allot some time in your daily routine to watch the desires that arise in your mind from morning till night with the understanding given in the above meditation.

6
The Problem Underlying All Problems

People used to approach a saint to find solutions to their problems. The saint would ask them to write down all their problems in multiples of ten like ten, twenty, thirty and so on.

If people listed ten problems, he would tell them, "I don't have the solution to any of your ten problems, but I have the solution to your eleventh problem!"

They would wonder, "Hey! Which eleventh problem is this – a problem that I myself do not know of?"

The saint would explain, "The eleventh problem is your desire to *not* have any problems in your life."

Like children, we have come to the earth school to give exams. Our everyday life situations are the exams that we need to solve to scale up to the next level. When we encounter certain situations in life, we may feel intimidated or we may take it as a challenge. A situation or an incident appears to be a problem when it is viewed through the lens of limiting beliefs. If we look at the so-called problems of our life from a detached perspective, they are opportunities for progress, the harbingers of growth and evolution.

Every so-called problem or challenge occurs in our life so that we develop our capability and unleash our potential. It prods us to develop qualities within us and manifests the next state of evolution in life.

When we learn, grow and make progress, we attain success in overcoming the challenge. Every success, in turn, brings with it the next level of challenges. So the cycle of growth keeps going this way:

Challenge >>> Progress >>> Success >>> Next challenge…

But just as children consider exams to be problems, our reluctant mind considers the uncomfortable situations in life to be problems. The moment it confronts a problem, it immediately reacts, "This must not happen… That must not happen…" This thought in itself becomes a problem as it gives the mind a means of troubling us.

But if you release the desire to *not* have any problems, then how would your life be? Declare that you let go off this desire, for problems will continue to come and go in your life, but you will not resist them. What is your role then? Your role is to find solutions to your problems.

Imagine someone hires you for a job. Your job is to find solutions to problems. Now whatever be the problem, you will engage yourself in solving it. In the earth school, you can consider that you have been hired by God to solve the problems of your life.

How will you perform this job? Won't you do it happily? As soon as you face a problem, you will consider, "God has assigned this problem to me. I will solve it."

When a company hires people, the company wants them to solve their problems. Similarly, if God has hired you to solve problems, then whose problems are they? They are God's problems. You have been hired by God to solve His problems. Then what's your problem? None of the problems belong to you. As you believed them to be yours, your mind desires not to have them and that in itself is a problem. Be happy to be hired by God to solve His problems!

Having understood this, imagine how your life will be? Whenever you face a problem, you will say, "Here is a problem given by God. Let me find a solution to this." You will look at problems in a new way like never before.

The solving of a problem will not bring you pain – it will bring you earnings! You will receive payments in Love, Joy, Peace and Fulfilment.

Now, we will look at how to deal with our thoughts, distance them using various techniques in the forthcoming chapters.

Action plan

- Look at the problems in your life with the understanding given above and write down your experiences.

7
Essence of Thoughts, Gravity of Intent

Have you ever wondered, what the essence of the thoughts that you entertain during your entire day could be? What has been the essence of your thoughts during this entire month? What has been the essence of your thoughts over this year?

Perhaps, you may not have thought about this so far. But the essence of your thoughts along with the accompanying emotions and your intention – all put together create your world. It is the orchestra of your thoughts, emotions and intentions that brings you the experience of your world.

So, how is your world today?

Not everyone's world is the same. Each one is carrying their own personalized world in their mind. So, there are as many worlds as the number of people.

We believe that the world exists outside us as we perceive everything outside. But the picture of whatever we see is developed inside. The retina gathers information from whatever our eyes see and sends it to the brain. The brain then processes the electrical impulses and renders an image. So is the case with sounds, tastes, aromas. To add to this, our mind associates whatever is being experienced with our past impressions and matches them, thereby conditioning or labelling whatever we experience.

Your world exists within you. Whether it is a happy world or a sorrowful one, joyous or troublesome – it is *your* world. If you want to change it for the better, you can do it. If you wish to have abundance, prosperity, love, joy, health, harmonious relations, then you can have the world that way.

> As a remedy to an ailment, a rich man was advised to only see green things everywhere by his doctor. As he could afford it, he painted his entire house, workplace and surroundings green. On seeing this, a wise man exclaimed, "Alas! You only needed to get spectacles with green glasses and it would have done the job."

If you want to change your world, what do you need to do for that? You need to change how you perceive the world. And your perception of the world can be changed when you embrace the principle of perception, which states – **The essence of thoughts and the gravity of intent create your world.** By understanding and applying this principle, you can change your experience of the world. Then your mind will not trouble you anymore.

Following the principle, we need to change the essence of our thoughts and the gravity of our emotions to transform our world. If we continue to think whatever we have for all these days, this transformation is not going to happen.

Let's understand what "essence of thoughts" means, with an example.

> Asha wanted to complete her project work but she didn't get access to a computer on time. Then there was a power failure. When the power was restored, her internet connection was not working. She needed help from her project leader to complete her draft, but he was not available.

If we consider the thoughts Asha entertained during these incidents, they were "Why does this happen with me alone? Why do things go wrong when I need them the most? Why do I need to depend on others? Why can't I do things on my own?" While she might not have used these exact words, the essence of her thoughts was – I am inadequate. I am not capable enough. I can't do this alone. Things never work for me.

Thus, the essence of her thoughts are the sum total of the underlying core beliefs that are deeply rooted in her mind. Her core belief could be – "I am not enough" or "I do not deserve."

If this is the essence of her thoughts, then how would her world be? She will encounter obstacles in whatever she does. In order to change her world, she needs to change her core beliefs to "I am enough. God has given me all the qualities that I require." With this, she will update and upgrade her mind.

With the passage of time, as a child grows, he gets upgraded. To start with, he cannot walk, but soon learns to walk. He cannot ride a bicycle, but soon learns cycling too. The child keeps learning rapidly. But after a certain age, the learning stops. He stops updating and upgrading himself. But why should it stop? Ideally, learning and upgrading should continue throughout one's lifetime.

In the context of our core beliefs, continuous learning is about bringing our core limiting beliefs to light and then replacing them with healthy beliefs that can improve our personal experience of the world.

So, if the essence of our thoughts is "I am not enough", our world gets created accordingly. If someone else doesn't have such thoughts, his work gets completed smoothly, without any hurdles. He may possibly get stuck in some other kind of thoughts, based on his set of core beliefs.

Each of us needs to examine our thoughts to unravel their essence. If the essence of someone's thoughts is "I am not likable", then his world mirrors that thought. He always thinks, "I am wretched. No one needs me. I am incomplete."

He needs to change his thoughts now and invite thoughts of completeness in him. The thoughts of completeness are "I am complete. I am enough. I am adequate. I am the source of love and attention." When he repeats these new thoughts, their essence creates a new world for him.

Passionately reflect on what you really want in your life instead of pondering about what you don't want. Be firm on what you want, set your emotions and intention on it. Have faith that God is leading you in that direction. This line of thinking helps you direct your mind, because it impregnates the mind with beliefs to create the best world. It is bereft of any wrong beliefs or erroneous convictions.

Let's understand what an erroneous conviction is. Indian tradition abounds in myths such as – Something bad will happen if a cat crosses one's path; If one's palm itches, one is going to receive money; The twitching of one's eye implies something bad will happen; One should not buy things on Saturdays; One should not wear black attire; This particular dress is lucky; All endeavors are successful when one wears a particular ring or adorns a particular gemstone.

One gets evidence of whatever one believes in. The belief then gets reinforced. One gets firmly convinced that this is how life works. If someone challenges their belief, they refuse to accept it. With this kind of repeated thinking, what is going to be their essence of thoughts?

People who are bugged by troublesome thoughts often think, "I cannot escape this mess. I am stuck." When this is the essence of their thoughts, it is bound to manifest in their life. They will be troubled in their life. If they want to carve a new life for themselves, they need to give new thoughts to their minds.

In order to understand the essence of your thoughts, you need to understand the thoughts that you entertain from morning till night. Let's practice a meditation to understand this. First read the instructions and then practice the meditation.

1. Before beginning, you may set a timer for ten minutes. You may use your cell phone, a computer, a clock or a watch for that.

2. Now sit in a comfortable posture for meditation and close your eyes.

3. In this meditation, as soon as a thought arises, say "Next". Wait for the next thought to arise and say "Next". Watch as your thoughts come and go. Without getting into their details, let them keep passing naturally. Some thoughts may be positive, some negative, some related to work while others still may be thoughts of boredom. Whatever be the thought, just say "Next".

4. Some thoughts about work or some important and urgent matter might distract your attention. Your mind might wander away and pursue a chain of thought instead of saying "Next". If this happens, whenever you remember, say "Next" and continue with your meditation.

5. Continue this till the timer goes off. Slowly open your eyes.

As soon as you close your eyes, countless thoughts flood your awareness out of nowhere. These thoughts were already present, but you were not aware of them. If you carefully observe them, you will understand your underlying core beliefs that form the essence of your thoughts.

In the next chapter, let's look at how the seeds of emotions affect the essence of thoughts.

Action plan

- Reflect on the essence of the thoughts that you entertain from morning to night. Consciously change them to what you really want in life.

8
Sow the Right Seeds of Emotions

We have seen how changing the essence of our thoughts is the key to changing our experience of the world. In order to change the essence of thoughts, we need to change the thoughts that we entertain from morning till night.

Our emotions have a vital bearing on our thoughts. Hence, we need to be careful about the seeds of emotions that we are sowing during each and every incident in our life.

> Anita would start feeling depressed whenever she heard a particular song. She would keep wondering, "I was fine just a short while ago. Why am I feeling so gloomy all of a sudden?"
>
> Anita reflected on this and realized that whenever she heard a certain kind of music, she felt depressed. This continued and over time it worsened to the extent that she started fearing such music and avoided it. To solve this problem, she started seeing a psychiatrist.
>
> During her sessions, they came to a realization. Anita's mother had died when she was a teenager. When her mother was being buried, the same music was being played somewhere near the burial. Due to this, she had subconsciously associated that music with the depression she had felt at that

> delicate time. As a result, whenever Anita heard that music, she would start feeling desolate.

The above example is a fact. The predominant emotions that we experience whilst going through the incidents in life get etched in our mind and we subconsciously hold onto them. These are the seeds of emotions. Some of them are sown during our childhood when we didn't have the maturity and understanding. Whenever we go through similar situations, these emotions get triggered and rise up to the surface of our awareness. We fail to understand why we suddenly feel gloomy or insecure or irritated.

You can imagine the kind of thoughts that could occur when such negative emotions surface. We will have all sorts of negative, depressing thoughts that will affect the essence of our thoughts and our experience of the world in turn. Hence, in order to create a better world for ourselves, we need to consciously change these seeds of emotions for the better.

> On a quiet Sunday, when you are at home alone, all of a sudden a sad memory from the past pops up in your mind, making you despondent. At that time, you feel that being sad is justified. However, by being sad, you reinforce the seeds of sadness for your future. Instead, you can choose to shift to a happy frame of mind. By being happy, you change your subconscious programming to handle such situations with happiness in the future.

You need to identify the seeds of emotions you are sowing in every situation. What is the nature of your feelings towards people, towards tasks, towards the changing season, towards the environment around you?

If you feel, "These people are incompetent. They are useless. They are posing hurdles in my progress. They don't deserve anything good," then you are sowing wrong seeds of emotions for yourself. They will bear fruit and shape your world accordingly. You will remain frustrated with people. You will keep feeling troubled by others' actions.

Seeds of emotions beget our future. If we don't keep a check on them at the right time, they can affect our health. Then instead of solving the root cause, we get embroiled in treating the symptoms, which takes a lot of our time. Hence, it is important to be sensitive at the point of the root cause itself when negative seeds of emotions are being sown. Firmly resolve to sow positive seeds instead of negative seeds.

The right seeds of emotions in the above scenario would be, "I am surrounded by competent people. People always cooperate and work in synergy with me. They are helping me progress towards my chosen goal. I wish all the best things for them. Let their lives be filled with health, wealth and contentment. Let there be an abundance of love, joy and peace in their lives."

Just by reading these lines, we feel positive. If we keep doing this from morning till night every day, we sow positive seeds for our bright and beautiful future. It will change the essence of our thoughts. From here onwards, consciously keep your intent clear – you will sow only positive seeds. See only positivity everywhere. Focus on the positive qualities of people instead of their shortcomings.

If you keep at it consistently, your being will begin to align with a higher positive frequency, thereby attracting positive things and positive people towards you. Your world will become a better place to live, because you would have changed your experience of the world.

Release the wrong seeds of emotions

Whatever seeds of negative emotions we have sown so far lie suppressed in certain parts of our body. It's as if they cling on to those parts of the body. We can take the help of color and breathing exercises to release them from our body.

Our breath serves as a bridge between our body and mind. It can thus act as a pipe which can help us release the emotions that lie within. While making dough, we knead it properly to make it soft. Similarly, we have to make use of our breath to loosen the clinging emotions that harm our body. Just like a blacksmith uses a blower to push air in and out of the furnace, we have to use our breath to push out all the clinging emotions. We can also visually fill our body with our favorite color to erase emotions.

Let's practice a meditation to release these emotions suppressed in our stomach using our breath and colors. We are going to release all the emotions that have accumulated in the stomach. We will visualize the emotions as stubborn grime sticking in the stomach and use our breath and our favorite color as cleansing agents.

At the outset, decide your favorite color, except for black. All colors except black are shades of light. Black is the absence of light. Hence, choose a color other than black that you like the most.

While inhaling, we will focus on the nose. As the breath travels to the stomach, the focus should shift to the stomach. When the breath is released, the stomach contracts. This complete unit from the nose to the stomach is similar to the blower used by the blacksmith. When we breathe in, it is as if air is being blown into the whole body.

Read through the instructions first and then practice the meditation.

1. Before beginning, you may set a timer for five to ten minutes. You may use your cell phone, a computer, a clock or a watch for that.

2. Sit in a comfortable posture and close your eyes.

3. Breathe in through the nose. Observe its effect on the stomach. Imagine that the stomach is getting kneaded like dough when the breath is taken in and given out.

4. Now shift your focus to the stomach. Tell yourself, "Fear has accumulated in the stomach and is sticking to the inner

walls. I am going to massage my stomach by expanding and contracting it." Imagine that with every expansion and contraction of the stomach, its muscles are softening, fear is melting down and getting released.

5. Concentrate on the breathing and stomach expansion-contraction. With every breath that goes out from the body, tell yourself, "Fear is getting uprooted and released. I am becoming fearless."

6. Now visualize that the stomach muscles are being kneaded to dilute the acid of hatred which has formed in the stomach. Keep kneading and you will observe that the acid is reducing.

7. Let breathing happen naturally. Don't do it forcibly.

8. Your focus should pass from nose to stomach and then back to the nose.

9. Feel that the stomach has softened. The hardness caused due to hatred and guilt is reducing. The rust of jealousy, grudges and envy is getting removed. The acid of hatred is melting away.

10. Visually spray the light of your favorite chosen color inside and around your stomach. This light has the property of healing. It is erasing all pent up traces of emotions from your stomach.

11. Tell yourself, "Each outgoing breath is pushing out all these emotions away from the body in the form of vapor. All stiffness is being removed. The cholesterol of ego is melting away. It is being softened first and then released through the breath."

12. If you feel tired, relax and sit calmly.

13. With each outgoing breath, let go. Fear, hatred, jealousy, all that is stuck is now getting released with every outgoing breath. Raise both hands and let go. Keep chanting, "Let

go... Let go..." Your stomach is now radiating the healing light of your favorite color.

14. With a complete victory over your emotions, take your hands down.

15. Slowly open your eyes.

Let's look at how we can keep our thoughts positive in and through all situations in the next chapter.

Action plan

- Identify the seeds of emotions you are sowing in every situation. What are your feelings towards people, towards tasks, towards the changing seasons, towards the environment around you? Wherever you catch yourself sowing negative seeds, write them down and try giving them a positive twist.

9
Change the Momentum of Your Thoughts

We have discussed the principle – "Essence of thoughts and seeds of emotions create your world." In order to apply this principle in our life, we need to inculcate the most precious habit of changing the cycle of our thoughts. We can realize the value of this habit only when we actually practice it. Let's understand this with an example.

> When Riya was scolded by her boss in the office, she was feeling so distraught that she kept brooding over it even after reaching home. "He will get it from me tomorrow. I won't spare him. How dare he scold me in front of everyone? Does he know the difficulties that I go through balancing home and work? Despite all these difficulties at home, I met the quarterly target only to listen to his criticism. Next time onwards, I won't unduly stretch myself. Let him get it done from others. Enough of volunteering for such work. He doesn't value his team members. Let's see how he gets the work done without me. Then he will realize my value."

When thoughts arise on a topic, we tend to churn over the same topic again and again. The process of continuously thinking about the same thoughts, which tend to be sad or dark, is called rumination. The more we ruminate, the more the thoughts get fueled and gain momentum. After a while, even if we want to break this cycle, the thoughts don't stop. They keep coming back again and again.

Rumination occurs in the false hope that one can solve the problem by ruminating over it. With some people, this habit of rumination goes to such an extreme that it severely impacts their mental health. They may get into depression or it can impair their ability to think and process emotions. They need to consult a physician or a psychiatrist and undergo medication.

The good news is that you can break this cycle of constant rumination by inculcating a new habit of deliberately shifting your thoughts to a different stream. You may find it difficult to shift to a different topic when the cycle has gained momentum. Hence, you need to shift it when it has just begun. The starting point is the weak point of the cycle when thoughts have just begun to arise after the incident and you are just beginning to feel a subtle sense of trouble or sorrow.

It is at this point that you can make the change most easily, with the least effort. Once the cycle begins to run at too fast a pace, it becomes very difficult to stop. It is therefore vital that you become aware of the unwanted cycle of thoughts at the very first instance. You must immediately shift the thought cycle to a different stream of thoughts. Intentionally take the mind onto another topic.

Shifting Focus

It is crucial to inculcate the habit of shifting focus to new topics in order to stop the momentum of unwanted thoughts. This might seem difficult in the beginning because one thought cycle is already running and has gained momentum. However, you must develop this habit of deliberately switching to another topic. It becomes easier with practice.

This does not mean that you shift focus to any topic at random. You need to consciously switch your thoughts to some constructive topics that will render you strength. Practice it initially with any thought cycle that kicks in, regardless of whether it is a negative thought cycle or not. As you shift to the new cycle of thoughts, eventually the old cycle of thoughts stops running without your notice. You will then see that the power of the unwanted cycle of thoughts is exhausted; and before you know it, that cycle has disappeared. Otherwise, people remain stuck in the unwanted cycle of thoughts long enough to get sick and begin having psychosomatic symptoms on their body. Their negative thoughts attract negativity in their lives.

> You may have often noticed that a catchy tune gets stuck in your mind and replayed incessantly. Even though you may wish to stop it, you cannot, unless you start playing another song in your mind. You need to deliberately switch over to another song. Soon, the earlier tune will stop playing in your mind without your notice. What did you do for this? You just played another song.

Let's again consider the case of Riya.

> Riya was unable to stop ruminating over her boss's rude behavior even after reaching home. If she were to inculcate the habit of shifting focus consciously, she would start thinking about what she could cook for her family. She could think creatively about preparing a new dish, thus charging herself positively instead of sulking over the earlier topic. With the new thought cycle, the old one could have vanished.

Timing is important when it comes to switching your thoughts. You must switch over to the new stream of thoughts at the starting point itself when the unwanted thoughts just start arising within you, well before they gather momentum. You have the best chance to change the topic at the start itself. But you won't be able to do it if you have not inculcated this habit.

To make it a habit, start practicing it with small incidents. Try it deliberately with any topic, just to see if it works. If you are able to do it successfully, it will be a wonder for you that the topic has really stopped bugging you. You will gain confidence in your ability to shift focus. When the mind will actually begin to trouble you, you can then shift your focus easily. The topic may keep coming back at you, but if you persistently shift focus, you will find that it becomes easier for you. Otherwise, if your focus is stuck at one place, all your thoughts will revolve around that topic alone.

Without this habit, the mind keeps flogging itself incessantly with the whip of negative thoughts. It is a common sight in India to see *hath-yogis*, who walk the streets, flogging themselves with a whip to earn quick money. Ruminating over negative thoughts is just like flogging yourself. If only the mind could be convinced that it is needlessly tormenting itself. If only it were made to stop its whiplashes, but how? By shifting the topic of focus.

As the mind switches to another topic, you can choose to repeat, "I am *dear* to God; no fear can touch me. I am made in the image of God; my success is assured." The more you repeat sentences like these, the more you regain poise.

In the earlier scene, the mind was troubled with fear and anxiety, "What would be the outcome if this happens? What if I don't get admission in the required faculty of my interest? What if the court litigation is stalled? What if my business doesn't take off?"

While you nimbly shift from one topic to another, which topic should you choose to switch to? You should switch to that topic which builds your inner strength and trust. When the mind is filled with thoughts of fear, uncertainty and anxiety, you get troubled. Your energy drains away. The feeling of hopelessness creeps in. But the moment you start repeating, "I am *dear* to God; no fear can touch me," you gain strength and trust. The moment you keep affirming, "I am made in the image of God; my success is assured," you feel assured about your future.

People commit the mistake of fighting with their thoughts. They try hard to resist their negative thoughts. They desire to not have those thoughts, but end up having more of them. They wish those thoughts should not occur to them, but by doing so they repeatedly recall the same thoughts and reinforce them. By resisting your thoughts, you actually focus on those very thoughts and unknowingly energize them.

In order to avoid committing this mistake, you must nip your thoughts in the bud itself. A stitch in time saves nine. When the cycle of negative thoughts has begun, remind yourself, "I am now on the path of flogging myself with the whip. I must stop this." Switch to the new topic that energizes and refreshes you.

When people, who are scared of dark places, begin to sense even the slightest fear, they must repeat in their mind, "I am *dear* to God; no fear can touch me; only faith can touch me."

Otherwise, people live in fear. They read some bad news in the newspaper and the cycle of fear-inducing thoughts begins. "Oh! This should not happen to me." Immediately repeat in your mind, "I am *dear* to God; no fear can touch me; only faith can touch me."

Keep repeating this at speed initially, until you find that your fear has slowly vanished. Fast repetition ensures that your mind doesn't get a chance to pull you back to the old topic. This is also the benefit of fast chanting of mantras so that you do not regress to the troublesome old topic.

As soon as the troublesome thought starts, you can start chanting a mantra. The mantra could be any words like "Aum", "Aum Namah Shivay", "Help", "Waheguru", or any other words that attune you to positive vibrations. You can chant the mantra aloud or in your mind as per the convenience. As you chant the mantra, you shift to positive vibrations.

With practice, you will realize that if you want to shift your focus anyway, then why not shift to topics that raise your awareness. You can learn to make it an opportunity to remember the divine qualities you want to develop. You can also start singing hymns or devotional songs. As you do this, you will begin to be filled with joy and wonder. Thus, the troublesome thoughts that were pulling you into the quicksand of sorrow, serve to uplift you.

The habit of shifting focus can also come to your rescue when there are arguments between people. You can put a stop to their arguments by going up to them and deftly changing the topic, perhaps even to something mundane.

> Consider two people are arguing over something at home. You wish to shift their focus. You ask one of them, "Hey! Has your amazon parcel arrived?" He may say, "No, it has not arrived yet." "Oh! How long will it take? It's been four days already!"

The topic has changed. You just asked a different question to one of them. The warring duo can move out of the argument and shift to the new topic. The stress suddenly gets diffused just by changing the focus. You can experiment with this habit in many areas but mainly for changing your own thoughts. Let's understand more about this habit in the next chapter.

Action plan

- Observe your thoughts for 10 minutes. For every thought, make sure that you shift the topic. You shouldn't invest more than 1 or 2 thoughts on a given topic. This may seem difficult to start with. But with practice, you will start enjoying this like a game.

- Identify the incidents in your daily life situations where you tend to think negatively. Consciously change the cycle of thoughts and focus on positive or neutral topics.

10

Reflect on Yourself

The habit of shifting focus is beneficial in many ways. The more we practice it, the more we reap its benefits. So far, we have discussed about shifting our focus to positive topics such as divine music, qualities or even neutral topics of the outside world. But now, we will understand how we can shift our focus within, into our inner world, for our internal growth. Let's understand it with an example.

> You are proud of being meticulous. But you notice that your children are not upto the mark. All their things lie scattered around the house. This is also the case with your friends and relatives. They don't get any of their things in place. You are troubled by thoughts like, "Why can't they be disciplined like me? I detest people who are disorganized and reckless." These thoughts start gaining momentum.

To stop this momentum of thoughts, ask yourself, "What are the aspects of my own life where I am not meticulous and organized?" With this thought, you turn within and reflect on yourself. You introspect, "Am I able to organize my thoughts in their appropriate slots in the cupboard of my mind? Am I able to accomplish all my work as planned? Do I pay adequate attention to my health? Do I make right use of my wealth? Do I perform my social responsibilities well in an organized way?"

When you really dig deep within yourself, you'll notice that you may perhaps be neglecting your physical exercise or diet. Your mind may be enmeshed with several clashing thoughts. The fact that you fret over others' recklessness shows that your own thoughts flow helter skelter without discipline. Perhaps, you may be trying to solve your office issues at home and your domestic problems at your office. Perhaps you may not be making optimal use of your wealth; you may be trying to escape your social responsibilities in challenging situations.

When you shift your focus inward and introspect, it can bring such truths about yourself to light that you will feel: When I am less than perfect in so many areas of my life, why do I get angry over the few aspects where the children or neighbors are imperfect? They are, in fact, serving as a mirror for me, showing me all those facets where I am committing similar mistakes.

> There was a dog that entered a hall of mirrors. The walls, floor and ceiling were reflecting mirrors. The dog spent some time inside and eventually came out injured, bleeding and said, "Everybody barked at me, but somehow I managed to defend myself."
>
> You can imagine what would have happened. What if you told that dog, "Stop barking. See what you've done to yourself. You have hurt yourself. You are the cause of your suffering."
>
> What would the dog say? He would have probably said, "Go, tell those cowards who are hiding inside. They are the ones who are barking and picking up a fight."

This may sound hilarious, but this is also our story! This is how the mind looks at the world. It sees its own reflections and reacts. It complains about how others are always wrong.

All the situations and people in the world serve as mirrors to us. The world is not as it appears to us. It is how our thoughts are; it is a reflection of the thoughts and perceptions that we hold within us.

You project your mental traits, unresolved emotions, and deficiencies upon the world. Therefore, what you see as the world is a reflection of what you project. People, situations, the weather – everything that you experience – are shaded by your perception and are projections of what is held deep within your mind.

You shape personalities for the people around you, by using building blocks present within your own mind. This happens on its own without your conscious awareness, and you end up criticizing people for shortcomings that are merely a projection of your own deficiencies. You experience your own unresolved emotions by unknowingly projecting them on people, so that it appears to you as though they are enacting or setting off those emotions.

You get lost in external details to such an extent that you don't realize they are only living pictures of what lies buried within your mind. External situations are not the cause, but rather a reflection of what you hold within.

Different people perceive the same situation in different ways – why is that so? It's because they are projecting or superimposing their own personal mental baggage on the same screen, and then watching the scene through their own personal mental filters that distorts the picture of reality.

If we are able to understand and accept this profound truth about life, then we would say, "If my family, friends and colleagues are not behaving according to my expectations, then instead of getting angry, I need to look deep within myself to see whether I am behaving and living up to my own expectations in all facets of my life."

Let's consider some other cases of complaints that we may harbor, which can be turned around for introspection.

> You feel the other person is being rude and egoistic. Your mind starts presenting evidence of past incidents where the person was rude and egoistic.

To stop this momentum of complaints and blame, ask yourself, "What are the areas where I am being rude and egoistic? In which facets of my life do people consider me rude or egoistic?" This will shift your focus onto yourself. You will reflect on yourself, your relationships and find those facets where you have been rude or egoistic.

If you are not convinced, then you can contemplate on how you may have appeared to be rude or egoistic due to some misunderstanding. You can then surmise that people may also be appearing rude or egoistic to you, due to reasons that you cannot fully understand. Thus, when you shift your focus within, you learn more about yourself.

> You complain that your subordinates are not committed. They don't complete their tasks on time. Your housemaid is not committed. She doesn't come on time regularly. She doesn't show up very often.

Ask yourself, "What are the areas where I am not committed?" If you keep complaining that others are not committed, it could possibly mean that somehow in certain facets of life, you are not committed to yourself. Since a lack of commitment is an issue from within, you project it on people and complain that most people aren't committed.

There are leaders who command enormous respect, love, and commitment from people. This is because these leaders are committed to themselves. They do not lack commitment. As a result, they do not see a lack of commitment in others; automatically people are committed to them.

> When you listen to some people, you think that they must control their words.

Now, shift your focus within and ask yourself, "In what situations do I need to control my speech? What are the situations where I first speak out and then repent?" When you shift your focus to yourself in this manner, you encounter your own reality. You stop ruminating over the defects in the other person. You realize that the other person lacks control over his words in one facet and you lack control over your speech in some other facets of life. Then why should you blame the other person at all? When you shift focus on yourself, you weed out the negative thoughts and gain insights about yourself.

> If you are upset that you don't get help from others, ask yourself, "In which facets of life am I not helping myself?"

It is a popular scene in classrooms. A teacher complains that the students refuse to listen, they just won't calm down and behave themselves. Yet, when these students attend the class of another teacher, they become obedient and receptive. None of them misbehaves. The difference here is not how the students are, but how the teacher feels within herself. The first teacher is not committed to herself, so others, including her students, don't take her seriously. The second teacher listens to herself and hence, her students listen to her!

What happens in the outside world is a mirror of what is inside. When someone takes you for granted, it is an opportunity for you to dive within and see where you take yourself for granted. You may be neglecting your health or what you exactly feel within. If you find this to be true, then stop taking yourself for granted. Change in the external world will automatically manifest as a result of the internal change.

When we look at the people and incidents of our life with the eyes of introspection, all the reasons for our suffering come to light. The same incidents that were upsetting us, will become the cause of joy. We'll no longer feel hurt or angry at people. When this happens, we would have indeed used our negative thoughts as stepping stones for our own growth. Instead of being victims of negative thinking, we can use them for our own introspection to know our hidden reality.

In the chapters till this point, we have considered various ways in which we can change our perception about situations, that help us cope with and overcome negativity.

The chapters that follow discuss various techniques to encounter the mind and shift our focus out of negativity, when we are in the midst of the storm.

Action plan

- Whenever you catch yourself complaining or blaming about someone's behavior, set aside some time to turn back the complaint on yourself. Reflect on how you may be behaving the same way in the physical, mental, social, financial or spiritual facets of your life.

PART 2

ENCOUNTERING THE **TROUBLED** MIND

11
Magic of Self-Talk

Abraham Lincoln was born into poverty. He encountered failure on numerous occasions during his life. He lost eight elections, failed twice in business and suffered a nervous breakdown. He could have quit many times, but being a champion, he never gave up. Instead, he consistently worked upon improving himself through deep reading, learning and self-reflection. His persistence paid off when he went on to be one of the greatest presidents in the history of the United States, leading the nation during the Civil war, abolishing slavery and strengthening the federal government.

During the time when Lincoln was president, Thomas Edison was growing up to become one of the most prolific scientists in history. His teachers had said he was "too stupid to learn anything." He was fired from his first two jobs for being "non-productive." So much for someone who went on to have more than 1,000 patents registered in his name! As an inventor, Edison made 1,000 unsuccessful attempts at inventing the light bulb. When a reporter asked, "How did it feel to fail 1,000 times?" Edison replied, "I didn't 'fail' 1,000 times. The light bulb was an invention with 1,000 steps."

What differentiates a winner from a loser is his positive self-talk. There are innumerable examples of people in sports, business, science, politics and defense, who didn't give up despite facing defeat. As a result, they persevered and were blessed with the sunshine of success in their lives.

When athletes narrow down at the finishing line with a micro gap between their compatriots, what matters is their self-talk. During the last over of a cricket match when both the teams are at par, their self-belief reinforced by their self-talk makes the difference between a win and a loss.

Self-talk is anything we tell ourselves, be it aloud or in our mind. We communicate with other people through spoken language, but with ourselves through self-talk. Self-talk is nothing but quiet communication with ourselves by way of the thoughts that run in our heads. So, self-talk is the communication we use within ourselves. It is important to practice saying the right things to oneself and others.

Feelings, thoughts, words and actions have a bi-directional influence on each other. While our feelings and thoughts determine our speech, it is also possible to alter our thoughts and feelings by consciously regulating what we tell ourselves in our minds.

If we use wrong words while talking to others, they immediately correct us. However, when we say wrong words to ourselves, there is no one to correct us. As we grow up, we learn the art of right conversation in the external world. However, most people never learn the art of effective self-talk due to two reasons:

1. They probably never realize the need to learn it.
2. They usually never come across anybody who has mastered this skill and can guide them.

It is vital that we engage in the right self-talk. It is only when we improve our self-talk that we can improve our relationships and achieve all-round self-development. That's the magic we possess within us.

Our self-talk can benefit from adopting a particular vocabulary wherein certain words must be emphasized and repeated and certain words must be avoided. In our conversations with others, we avoid abusive or negative words to maintain harmonious relationships. Likewise, we need to cast away negative thoughts in order to sustain harmony and a healthy relationship with ourselves.

Punctuation plays an important role in self-talk. We must know where to insert a comma, or where a full stop is required. Good self-talk lets us communicate correctly with ourselves and maintain our peace. This positivity then gets reflected in our behavior towards others. Perfect communication is about having good self-talk and good use of speech.

Everyone wants to be free of their miseries, but they believe the cause of their miseries lies outside. But the real cause is their self-talk. If they work on their self-talk, the essence of their thoughts will automatically change to a positive one. Understanding the following principles can help in developing the right self-talk:

1. No incident is joyous or sorrowful in and by itself. Feelings of joy or sorrow stem from the self-talk that happens within your mind at the time of the incident.

2. You create your world with your self-talk. The root of all sorrow is nothing but your self-talk. Your self-talk creates heaven or hell for you.

3. Nobody can make you unhappy unless you allow them.

4. Just as man's difficulties exist within him, so do solutions.

5. Negative self-talk generates negativity in you. That negativity in turn flows into your communication with others, through your expressed feelings and words. Even if you constrain your feelings and self-talk about others, it does get communicated at the level of the subconscious mind.

The self-talk we engage in after every incident becomes a cause for joy or sorrow. If our self-talk is positive, like "I can surely do this", "I am going to win", "I have more than enough" we will see it manifesting in our life. However, if our self-talk is negative, like "I am going to fail", "I always mess up", "I don't deserve the good things", "I have a shortage of money" we see its consequences in our life. We then reinforce our beliefs based on these proofs and they continue to manifest in our life.

You may wonder what difference it would make if you have an intermittent negative self-talk. But it does really matter. With constant negative self-talk, we get into a spiral of negative thinking. These negative thoughts gain so much momentum that it becomes our reality. This in turn makes us more anxious and stressed. If it's not treated in time, we may get into a spiral of depression.

No one wants to lead a life in misery. Everyone aspires to have a life of peace, bliss, love, health and prosperity. They wish to have harmonious relations. For that, they need to work on their self-talk.

Whenever you become aware of negative self-talk going on in your head, intentionally change it to a positive one. How can we reframe our negative thoughts into positive ones in testing situations? Let's learn more about this in the next chapter.

Action Plan

- Whenever time permits, reflect on your ongoing self-talk and write it down. This will help you change it for the better.

12
Reframe Your Self-Talk

Daniel graduated in mechanical engineering with first class honors. He went to Sweden for his MS in Renewable energy. Although Renewable energy had not yet picked up so well in the market, he chose to go ahead with it as he was passionate about it and it was the undisputable future in a world of depleted natural resources. His parents also supported him by mortgaging their house to fund his studies. After passing out in flying colors in his post-graduation, he tried hard to secure a job, but to no avail. He came back to his parents and prepared himself for interviews.

Initially, he was very optimistic about job opportunities and applied to a number of companies. But some of the companies rejected him outright due to lack of working experience and others asked him to hold on for some time but didn't come back despite follow-ups.

Six months into job-seeking, Daniel didn't know what exactly went wrong. "I have excelled in academics. My attitude and aptitude is remarkable. Why am I not getting a job? Did I make a wrong choice by specializing in Renewable energy? Why didn't I enquire about the future prospects of this subject before seeking admission? All my schoolmates have already secured good jobs, then why not me? Either I don't get an interview call, or if I do, then they find reasons to deny me. I am a failure. I can't even help my parents repay the loan."

Peer pressure, stress and anxiety started building within him. His sleep patterns and hunger got disturbed. He stopped exercising regularly. Whoever met him would enquire about his job. Hence, he started avoiding meeting people and preferred to be alone at home. His parents were disturbed by his behavior. Earlier, they were keen about his job, but now they too had become more anxious about his wellbeing.

You might have seen many such Daniels in everyday life or you might perhaps have been a "Daniel" yourself. In today's fast paced life, everyone is subject to this fiercely competitive life where they feel stressed all the time. At any time of the day, there is something that is worrying them, if not consciously, then as an undercurrent at the subconscious level.

A student undergoes stress when he is unable to concentrate on his studies, cope with the demanding syllabus, or meet his parents' expectations in scoring good marks in exams. Even after passing out with flying colors, just like Daniel in the above example, one can experience stress in acquiring a job.

In such situations, people are not able to invest time in learning how to train their minds, so as to give their thoughts a direction. Slowly, the stress and worry induces a negative perspective in them. They become habitual negative thinkers. They tend to focus on negatives in almost every situation.

When one looks at everything with a negative perspective long enough, they feel a sense of worthlessness and futility. This feeling naturally affects their daily life. Their behavior causes distress to their family too. Hence, in order to hit the root cause, it's required to change their negative perspective. For that, they need to change their negative thoughts to positive ones.

As children, we used to give equal attention to both negative and positive thoughts. However, as we grow up, we tend to gravitate towards negative thoughts. For some reason, negative thoughts seem to linger in our minds and we spend more time with them. While we give negative thoughts all our attention, the positive ones get neglected. Gradually negative thinking becomes a habit. Negativity seems like the only viable option.

Imagine a person with a missing tooth. Only one out of his 32 teeth is missing and yet his tongue keeps going to the one that is missing, not the remaining ones that are intact. This is a natural tendency. Likewise, it becomes a natural tendency for a person to look at the negative in any situation, no matter how many positives he may be surrounded by. As a result, life becomes listless and the person succumbs to depression; sometimes so much that one starts to get thoughts of self-sabotage and suicide.

For such a person, diverting their attention from negative thoughts and focusing on positive thoughts would seem impossible. What was effortless during childhood becomes nearly impossible when one has grown up. However, when the person wakes up to the damage that negativity is doing to their life, they are compelled to rethink and attune to positivity.

Remember that negative thoughts are like weeds. They grow anywhere without any supervision or efforts. You will never have to work to get negative thoughts. Positive thoughts, on the other hand, are like a flourishing lush green farm. One has to work hard at it, purposefully sow good seeds, give ample water and fertilizer with constant care and attention. It is only by committing oneself and following up with hard work that one can develop the positivity that is necessary for a fulfilling life. Positivity is a habit that has to be carefully cultivated like a healthy crop. One has to consciously plant the seeds of positivity, else weeds of negativity will flourish naturally.

To sum up, one has to redirect one's attention from negative to positive thoughts. Cultivate the habit of generating positive thoughts and make positivity a way of life. Every time old thought patterns try to sneak back, one should remind oneself that it is only positivity that is the key to happiness, negativity will only lock the doors to a better future. The sooner one grasps this, the easier one can step out of the darkness of anxiety and despair.

There are techniques of converting negative thoughts to positive ones; we will consider the technique of Reframing here. You may try a combination of multiple techniques for yourself depending on your specific situation.

Whenever a negative thought arises, it gives rise to sorrow. With the technique of Reframing, you can immediately give a positive twist to the negative thought, giving you a positive feeling. Also, what may work for you need not exactly work for someone else. A particular reframed sentence may change your feelings; but it's not necessary that it will change some other person's feelings. Some other sentences may work for them. Therefore, the reframing which creates a positive feeling within you is specifically apt for you.

Let's reframe the negative thoughts that Daniel had.

Daniel's Negative Thoughts	Re-framed Thoughts
My attitude and aptitude are remarkable. Then why am I not getting a job?	My attitude and aptitude are remarkable. I may not be getting a job right now, but my future is assured! And the future can come any time, even in the next moment.
Did I make a wrong choice by graduating in Renewable energy?	My choice of graduating in Renewable energy was perfect based on the information available to me at that time. What is right for me will surely unfold at the right time.

Why didn't I enquire about the future prospects of this subject before seeking admission?	Nothing is fixed. Everything changes with time. Even this shall pass away. I have complete faith that the right opportunity will knock at my door at the right time. Let me prepare myself in the meantime.
All my schoolmates have secured good jobs then why not me?	If jobs have come to my schoolmates, it will surely come to me as well. Let me happily wait for some more time.
I am not good enough.	It may seem that I am not good enough but I am surely better off than many others. I am blessed with wonderful supportive parents. I am blessed to have good health. (Count your blessings here.)
Whenever I face any interview, I don't get selected.	I am not getting selected now because a better opportunity according to my divine plan awaits me and it is bound to come my way.
I am a failure.	Failure is a stepping stone to success. It is helping me prepare better for a brighter future.
I can't even help my parents repay the loan.	Very soon I will get a good job and repay the loan within no time.

So, how did you find the reframed thoughts? Did it change your feeling? It is a wonder how our feelings can change just by changing the choice of our words.

We make use of words to express our feelings, not just to others, but also to ourselves. The words that we use to describe our experience set the stage for our future experience and it becomes our reality. In short, whatever we describe, gets prescribed in our lives! How we communicate with ourselves directly impacts our experience of life.

Let's understand it with one more example.

> Amit was a teenager. He followed a particular pattern to store his friends' contacts on his mobile. A friend whose name was "Sagar" was stored as "*Mad* Sagar". He prefixed a tag word – an adjective – generally associated with the behavior of the friend, along with the name. So Sagar was tagged as "*Mad*". Whenever Sagar would call him, his first reaction would be, "Oh! The mad fellow's calling. Now he will speak all kinds of insane things."

What does Amit need to do in order to change his feelings? He needs to reframe his self-talk. What if he were to store Sagar's contact with the tag "Smile"? The next time when Sagar calls him, he can have a smile on his face. He will remember that whatever Sagar says, will not dent his happy mood. However crazy his friend's chatter would be, he would not get irritated. The mobile would provide the trigger for Amit at the very beginning of the call.

A homemaker, who used to often worry, used this technique innovatively. When her husband and children were away from home and would call her, she would be gripped by fear and anxiety… "Oh! Why are they calling out of the blue? Is something wrong?" We experience this many a times. When the phone rings in the middle of the night, many people get anxious and worried, "Why now?" The mind begins to experience fear, "What's wrong?"

This lady knew she would keep experiencing this fear. So what did she do? She stored her son's name on her mobile as "Love", her husband's name as "Joy", and her father's name as "Peace". Now whenever she receives calls from them, her mobile flashes the message, "Love calling…", "Joy calling…", "Peace calling…". She feels elated looking at them. This also serves as a reminder for her to check her feelings. Thus, we can make use of gadgets to serve us reminders.

So, if we want to have a life that is filled with positivity and better quality, what do we need to do? Start describing it with positive words that are carefully chosen. Consciously switch the negative self-talk into positive self-talk by reframing your negative thoughts and you will notice that your feelings will automatically change.

As you start having positive thoughts, you become open to all the positivity in the universe. New ideas start flowing through you. These new thoughts and ideas have the potential to bring transformation in your life. Soon, you will see the life you aspire for turning into reality.

In situations where you are unable to reframe your self-talk, use the mantra of acceptance. When you are able to accept the situation or person in front of you, your mind calms down and you are able to shift to positive self-talk. Let's understand more about the mantra of acceptance in the next chapter.

Action plan

- List down the negative thoughts that frequently bog you down and reframe them to positive ones. Note the change in your feelings.

13
Magic of Acceptance

Leena worked as an investment consultant with a leading financial institution in Mumbai. Her son, Mihir, was doing his MS at Boston in the United States. Leena was looking forward to take a break and spend a couple of months with Mihir during his summer vacation. She made all the necessary travel arrangements and also got her leave sanctioned.

But just the day before her travel, she met with an accident and dislocated her shoulder. She was advised strict bed rest and travel was ruled out. Leena was in a state of shock. She wasn't able to accept that this had happened to her. She was filled with anger and despondency at the sudden turn of events.

When many of us go through such situations, we tend to blame the situation or the people around us. If there is no one else to be blamed, we blame ourselves for our carelessness and keep grumbling. We analyze to find the root cause of the problem. But the more we analyze, the more our thinking process can get paralyzed. We find ourselves in the quicksand of sorrow and guilt. With this mindset, we become closed to any input. Finding a solution to our problem becomes far-fetched.

We will now consider a technique that is profound and immensely effective. The utter simplicity of this technique is so striking that it can be a challenge for the mind to accept its relevance and efficacy!

In life we come across many undesirable situations that cause us great misery. Even trivial incidents make us retreat into our shell and feel unhappy. What can we do at such times when whatever is happening, or has happened is frustrating and disagreeable?

At such times, to emerge from this mental standoff, we can consciously ask ourselves, "Can I accept [this]?" Here "this" implies whatever is happening at this particular moment. It could be something that is affecting us either outside in the world or within us in the form of thoughts, feelings or body sensations.

Though it may not seem like it, "Can I accept this?" is nothing short of a magic mantra! The proof of the pudding is in the eating. So the efficacy of this mantra lies in actually applying it in testing situations, which are disagreeable.

Acceptance is the most natural and powerful approach to calm the mind and bring it into a constructive frame. It is important to understand why this is so. Understanding the "why" of acceptance is more relevant than getting into the details of "how" to accept.

All the sorrow and stress that we feel in life can be attributed to one single reason – Resistance. When we resist any situation, person, or incident, we are hampering the natural flow of life. When water stagnates in a pond, it gives out a foul smell, germs breed in the water, making it unhygienic.

Similarly, when we put up resistance and try to stop incidents from happening in our lives, the misery and the negative thoughts get an enclosure called "Resistance" to stay inside.

What does Resistance do?

When we cringe or withdraw in an undesirable situation, we enclose ourselves and the misery remains within us. This breeds germs like anger, boredom, comparison, fear, guilt, hatred, jealousy and resentment within us. These emotions consume a lot of our energy for their survival and in turn, we experience stress, anxiety and sadness.

In addition to these infesting emotions, the resisting mind also gets clouded with bias and a restricted view. With the clutter of thoughts that resistance creates, it is difficult to think clearly and creatively, making it impossible to bring the most suitable solutions for the situation.

Now, what can Acceptance do?

Accepting whatever is, dissolves the resistance, allowing the pent up emotions and negative thoughts to be released. Not just that, acceptance also enables us to organize our thoughts and think more clearly. It clears the lens of our perceptions, making us more capable and open to solutions that we could not have otherwise thought of.

Accepting the situation does not mean that you should follow what others dictate to you. It just simply means accepting it. As you accept it, the whirlpool of thoughts in your mind calms down. You feel relaxed and capable to think of a solution.

Taking a simple example from daily life, resisting a situation is like trying to tie shoelaces with just one hand while arresting the movement of the other hand. It becomes difficult. Accepting the situation is like freeing both hands and tying shoelaces!

In the case of Leena, when she asks herself, "Can I accept not travelling to US?" her ability to tackle the situation is enhanced to a great degree. The moment she accepts the situation, she will be open to the idea of rescheduling her trip in the best possible way by weighing the circumstances.

Leena gives priority to recovering from the injury and regaining her fitness first. She makes necessary changes in her travel itinerary as advised by the doctor.

This little mantra can work wonders. When you ask yourself, "Can

I accept this?" in most situations, you will get "Yes" for an answer. The moment the mind gets into the frame of agreement, you will no longer find yourself withdrawn or closed. This enables you to relieve yourself from the clutter of resisting thoughts and think with an open mind. Solutions come to those who are at ease and peace.

You can use this mantra in various situations ranging from severe to trivial ones. Following are some example scenarios:

- You have put in efforts to accomplish a task and your colleague gets all the appreciation for that. You get furious.
- You have committed a deadline to your client and your subordinates don't turn up for work. Your stress builds up.
- You need to submit your assignment and your computer crashes.
- You greet someone, "Good morning" and the other person ignores you.
- You are about to take a shower and the water stops.
- An important family function coincides with your client's meeting. You don't want to disappoint your family but you can't avoid the client meeting either. Finally, you decide to skip the function but your mind is frustrated with thoughts of anger and helplessness.

In most cases, when you ask yourself, "Can I accept this?" the answer will be "Yes". However, in situations where it is "No", ask yourself, "Can I accept this non-acceptance?" Suppose someone has insulted you and you are unable to forget it. Your mind constantly ruminates over the matter and provokes you to get even with him. In such a situation, if you cannot accept what has happened, then you can at least accept your non-acceptance. You can accept the fact that it is not acceptable to you right now. Come to terms with the non-acceptance. After some time, ask yourself again, "Can I accept this?"

You will find that invariably you will be able to accept the situation.

But does accepting the situation mean that we are not doing anything about it?

Not at all! On the contrary, it is only from a mental frame of acceptance that wise action can arise. The energy that was consumed in the flurry of negative thoughts due to non-acceptance gets freed with acceptance and we feel relieved from stress. Energy gets directed towards creative and wise decision making. We get flooded with new ideas to solve the problem. We find ourselves in more control and feel confident. Thus, by accepting the situation we get empowered to work on the solution more effectively and efficiently.

Most children forget and move on quite quickly after an unhappy scene. When we were children, we were able to accept undesirable incidents. Life was like a stream of free flowing water. We were bubbling with joy and rejoicing every moment. But as we grew up, we got conditioned with beliefs and fixations like, "This should be done", "That shouldn't happen." We then started evaluating every situation through the lens of these conditioned beliefs. This has created resistance within us, binding us to the shackles of sorrow. Due to this, life can seem like a misery for us. We may even look at every incident as a hurdle in life and wonder, "Why are these thoughts coming to my mind? When will I get free from them?"

Apart from external situations, there are many people who face resistance from within. They find it difficult to accept themselves. They keep lamenting about their gender, parents and country. A girl may feel, "I should have been born a boy." A boy may feel, "I should have been born to a rich family in a developed country." They need to ask, "Can I accept myself exactly as I am?" When one gets a "Yes" for an answer, the mind will calm down.

As we make use of the mantra of acceptance, the shackles of sorrow diminish. We become more capable of having a positive self-talk. This in turn has a positive effect on the essence of our thoughts and sows positive seeds for a better life.

In order to get into a frame of accepting whatever is happening, it's essential that we become alert and aware when negative thoughts begin. Depending on the kind of situation, we need to cajole the mind into acceptance by using various modalities. Let's understand them in the next chapter.

Action Plan

- Identify the areas in your everyday life where you experience resistance. Write them down. Make use of the mantra of acceptance in these situations.

14

Modalities for Acceptance

We have seen how acceptance calms the mind and opens it to possibilities. Situations can vary, incidents can play on our minds in various ways. Hence, it helps to understand the situation and tackle the negative self-talk and apply an effective modality so as to bring the mind into a frame of acceptance.

In our daily life, we come across situations where we were supposed to get something that we were looking forward to, but didn't.

Suppose you go to someone's place and they don't offer you tea. Or you propose a solution in a meeting but no one pays heed to you. Or they take a decision without informing you. Or your favorite team loses a match against its archrival.

At such times, we feel incomplete, frustrated, dejected or unworthy. We feel that we can be happy only if we could get that thing.

Now consider some worrisome thoughts that can pop-up and trouble you. "What will happen if I go broke? What will happen if I don't get a job? What if no one appreciates me or acknowledges my contribution? What will happen if I put on weight? What will happen if I don't score well? What if I fall sick? What will happen to me if I am left alone? What will I do if my friends and relatives are upset with me? How will I survive with the rising inflation? What will happen if I don't find the perfect life partner? What if I am never able to visit any other country?" This list can go on...

These small but trivial worries consume a lot of our energy. With every such incident or worry, our mind grumbles, "This shouldn't happen." This builds resistance within us and raises the momentum of negative thoughts. We lose peace. If we don't keep a timely check on them, they can lead us to depression.

At such times, we can use the mantra, "It Doesn't Matter." These three words serve like a mantra to help us come out of the negative spiral. It is one of the modalities of acceptance for situations where the mind resists a possibility.

When we find that we are unable to shake off negative thoughts, we can keep repeating this mantra. It serves as a force-technique to pull the mind out of the quicksand of negative thoughts.

Let's understand how we can use this mantra in our day-to-day life with some examples.

> When someone ridicules you, you feel bad. But the moment you say, "It Doesn't Matter," even if you may not necessarily stop feeling bad about, you will at least feel some respite. You will be able to accept the other person's behavior.

> Whenever you don't like someone's response, you naturally grumble, "Why didn't he respond properly? Why does he always have to act that way?" However, the moment you say, "It Doesn't Matter," you open yourself to a new perspective.

Just as we had discussed in the previous chapter, when we resist a situation, it's like building banks along the river of unhappiness. This in turn deepens the river leading to accumulation of more suffering. When we use this mantra, we remove the banks and let the suffering spread away and vanish. The problem becomes fluid and begins to dissolve. We can experience some relief, if not happiness. Otherwise, the more we resist, the more unhappiness accumulates, leading to heaviness and gloom.

We can also use the "It Doesn't Matter" mantra in situations where we lack clarity; where our view is clouded. Leave aside the problem for some time. In a few days, you will be able to get some insight on the solution to your problem. It may come to you through some person, thought or some piece of information. You will then find a new way of solving it.

Just as milk for the young one is arranged even before it's born, similarly the solution to every problem is already present. You need to earnestly believe that the solution to your problem is already present. You only need to get your mind into a relaxed state and you will be able to access the solution.

Many great scientists and inventors have used this method, knowingly or unknowingly. They were in the middle of trying to solve a stubborn problem but kept hitting the wall. So, they set aside the problem for some time. While their mind was unoccupied, the solution would suddenly emerge intuitively.

The same thing applies in all areas of life. When you are unable to find a solution to your problem, it is better to keep it aside for some time. The solution could hit you at the most unexpected moments when you are relaxed, taking a shower, taking a stroll in the park, or during some mundane conversation. Even a little hint can lead you to the solution.

For example, if someone is unable to find a job, then by pondering it repeatedly, his thinking process comes to a standstill and he begins to feel despondent. But the moment he says, "It Doesn't Matter", he stops resisting the situation. He remains in the present moment and becomes receptive for the slightest of indications. His chances of stumbling upon the solution goes up considerably.

"It Doesn't Matter" – these three miraculous words help us to become stress free. But the mind doesn't really take long to be entangled again. Hence, it's necessary to repeat "It Doesn't Matter" several times a day in order to be free from any entanglement of the mind.

Just as we regularly clean the dust accumulated on the various objects in our house, we need to keep cleansing our mind. Whenever the mind starts thinking negatively, it starts gathering the dust of sorrow. Repeating this simple mantra can help declutter the mind.

Overcoming the exaggerations of the troubled mind

> Meena was a homemaker. She was obsessed about having everything spick and span. Even if she would spot dust on the furniture, she would make a great hue and cry about it and shout at people. Her family was fed up of her habit.

It is a common trait to make a mountain out of a molehill. People with this trait tend to magnify things that are not really critical and give them undue importance. When things do not turn out as they would like, resistance builds up within them. Gradually they start fretting. When they are served a full delicious meal, their focus zooms in on a tiny aspect that puts them off. As a result, they ignore the sumptuous food… being grateful is farfetched for them.

When everything else goes well in their life, they focus on the trivial things that are not happening and brood. It is a law of nature that whatever you focus on grows in your life. Hence, they get to see even more negative incidents happening in their life.

There is a saying that the fear of calamity is much more grave than the calamity itself. Actually, all incidents happen spontaneously and naturally in life. But the mind can blow things out of proportion and present them in a magnified way. This can cause turmoil over trivial matters.

To apply a break on this habit of the mind, contemplate on the incidents that you have exaggerated in the past. Ask yourself, "Am I giving these incidents an exaggerated value than what they actually deserve?"

During the incident, if we ask ourselves, "What's the worst that can happen here?" we'll realize that we were having an exaggerated view. Tell yourself, "Oh, it's not a big deal!" The mind then stops its churning.

"Not a Big Deal" – just saying this to yourself in an emphatic manner can lead the mind out of its exaggeration. Let's understand its application in daily life with some examples.

1. When school students are assigned more homework than usual and there is a time crunch, they feel stressed and cannot figure out how to go about their work. At such times, they can tell themselves, "Not a Big Deal! All students have got the same homework." The moment they verbalize this, they can come out of the troubled state and immediately get to work to complete their homework effectively.

2. When one gets into arguments with the other person, one's mind starts its chatter and messes up everything. For example, a person has a fight with his brother. Being disappointed, he says, "My brother always behaves unjustly. Just because he is older, it doesn't mean he should always dominate me. He has no right to behave in such a manner." At such a time, the "Not a Big Deal" mantra can come to his rescue. Just by saying this mantra he can allay his negative thoughts and attain peace and harmony.

3. When a person suffers from memory loss, he feels dejected. He concludes that he is getting old and the brain is wearing out. Despite repeated attempts, when he fails to remember anything, then things begin to look bleak. At such times, he should use "Not a Big Deal" mantra and leave things aside. There is a possibility that after sometime, he may recall those things and come out of his troubled state of mind.

Taking a cue from these examples, we can use these mantras in our daily life to set aside depressing thoughts. However, one may question, "Are we running away from our problems by just saying 'It Doesn't matter' or 'Not a Big Deal'?" The truth is actually the contrary. This is not escapism, but a clever way of directing the mind towards constructive solutions. Let's understand this with an example.

Karan wanted to complete his project work. He had to make three hundred corrections in a month. It was a humongous task, which he felt was impossible. But he used the mantra, "Not a Big Deal." With this, his mind calmed down and became open to new creative ideas.

Then he divided the problem into smaller units. At first, it was a huge problem – three hundred corrections to be done in one month. Then he thought, "This actually means that ten corrections need to be made each day. Two before breakfast, three after breakfast, three before dinner and two after dinner… and the problem was solved! Solved without even needing extra time." When he actually worked upon his plan, he could complete the project work in time with quality.

Karan's troubled mind wouldn't have made it possible for him to complete his project work. But when he used the mantra, his mind quietened and he could think of new ways of solving the problem. The moment the daunting problem was divided into segments, it no longer remained big.

In the next chapter, we will understand what we can do when the mind dwells in the future and doesn't allow you to remain in the present.

Action plan

At the end of each day:

- Recall minor incidents during the day, which have caused despair. For each of these incidents, tell yourself, "It Doesn't Matter."
- Also recall those thoughts that trouble you or make you anxious. Tell yourself, "It Doesn't Matter."
- Contemplate the incidents that you tend to exaggerate and get troubled about. Apply the "Not a Big Deal" mantra.

15

Bother Then, When Then Becomes Now

Nisha was worried about securing admission for her son Sumit in a reputed school next year. She appointed a tutor for Sumit so as to prepare him for the entrance exams. Although Sumit was finding it tough to go through the syllabus, Nisha insisted that he had to. If he didn't get selected for the school, it would be a matter of social embarrassment for her. Both Nisha and Sumit were stressed.

This happens with most parents when they seek school admission for their children. The little children are unable to cope with the stress they are put to. The parents also excessively worry in advance about whether their children will get the admission in the reputed schools. They make this a matter of social pride. If their child fails to get admission, they consider it a social embarrassment.

People spend an inordinate amount of time and energy pondering, "When this particular thing happens, I shall act in this manner." In other words, instead of being in the present moment which is the only real moment of opportunity, they dwell in the worries of the future and become anxious. Chronic worrying and anxiety about the future leads to depression.

When you find yourself obsessing over the future, remind yourself, "Bother then, when 'then' becomes now." This is not a mere statement; it is a mantra that carries a powerful perspective which is very effective in keeping stress and depression at bay.

"Bother then, when 'then' becomes now" – this is no less than a grand aphorism for life. We need to contemplate deeply to understand the perspective that it presents. But once understood, these words can help you stay anchored in the present during challenging times.

"Bother then, when then becomes now," means that we do not need to fret about the future and miss out on the joy of the present. When the then (future) eventually arrives in the now (present), we will bother about what is to be done. We will bother about the future when it comes; for now, we stay in the present and witness the moment. This is all that we need to do to be at peace and in joy.

It takes just a fraction of a second for a thought to pop up in the mind, but we spend hours mulling over it. Let's understand how we can use this mantra with some examples.

1. Samir received a call from his boss on Friday evening. The boss told him, "Come and meet me in my office on Monday morning as soon as you are in." Now Samir keeps pondering, "Why does the boss want to see me? That too, first thing on Monday morning! Am I in for trouble? Have I messed up? Are they firing me?"

    He scanned through his activities over the past few weeks and tried to find where he could have gone wrong. The more he analyzed, the more anxious he felt. He cancelled his weekend plans, including the birthday dine out that he had planned with his family. While worrying about what would happen, he missed out on the little joys that he could have experienced in the present.

    Excessive thinking is like a depression booster. It kills enthusiasm. It sucks out the positive energy and renders the person hopeless and low-spirited. In order to apply brakes on his excessive thinking, Samir could remind himself, "I will bother about this when it's Monday morning at the office." With this, his obsession over the future could subside and he would remain in the present moment. He would enjoy the weekend with his family and feel happy about it.

2. While studying for his exams, Rohan kept worrying, "What if I don't score good marks? What if I don't get placed in a good company? Will I get an opportunity abroad like my friends? How will I fulfil my responsibilities? What if I'm not able to earn and take care of my family?"

Due to these apprehensions, Rohan was anxious and stressed, unable to focus on his studies. Had he used the mantra, "I will bother about my job when the time comes. Let's bother then, when then becomes now," it would have helped him remain in the present and effectively focus on his studies. All the excess thoughts would have then subsided. By being attuned with the present, he could have remained contented and at ease, attracting positivity in his life.

3. One morning, Harry realized that he was late for settling his credit card bill. He kept worrying, "What if my card gets blocked? I need to take my wife out to buy a refrigerator tomorrow. Darn! This had to happen today! What's the late fee they will charge me?" Harry's mind frequently kept fretting about this, making him angry and forlorn.

Harry should apply the mantra, "I will bother about this then, when then is now." This will enable him to take the necessary actions required in the present. Clearing the credit card bill would be the most logical and urgent action in this case, after which there would be no reason left for Harry to worry. Simple as it sounds, people often ignore the most obvious actions and instead choose to obsess and worry.

Sometimes, the mind resists being in the present. It gravitates towards problems that lie in the far future. At such junctures, tell the mind, "Cross the bridge when it comes. You can think about the problems that could arise within the next three months." Once the mind agrees to this, then bring it down to topics that need attention in the next week, then the next couple of days.

Slowly, a time will come when you will decide a fixed time slot for worrying about problems. You will tell the mind, "Let's worry about it at 6 p.m." And when it is 6 p.m., you will see that you won't worry, even if you wanted to. Instead, you would choose to spend that time doing something worthwhile.

> If a boxer were to wear his boxing gloves day and night, a week before the fight, you would tell him, "Why are you wearing your gloves so soon? Wait for the day of the fight. It will make sense to wear your gloves then, just before you enter the boxing ring!"

The present moment is a goldmine of joy that won't just make you happy, but will also empower you to spread happiness to those around you.

Let's practice a meditation to experience the bliss of the present moment. First read the instructions and then practice the meditation.

1. Before beginning, you may set a timer for ten minutes, You may use your cell phone, a computer, a clock or a watch for that.

2. Now sit in a comfortable posture for meditation and close your eyes. Closing of eyes helps focus on what is here and now.

3. Take a few breaths, exhaling slowly.

4. Ease your breathing to a gentle rhythm and begin to count each breath. Assign a running number to each incoming breath. If you lose the sequence in between, just start afresh with a new series.

5. Continue this till you reach the count of twenty.

6. With your eyes closed, take yourself into the experience of what's right here, right now… where there is no past and no future.

   You are sitting in a state where there is no thought of the future. The future does not exist. There is no need to get up and go anywhere. No activity to be done in the future. You are here forever.

   Nothing is going to happen. You need not even open your eyes to see anything. Not even the need to get up in the future.

   This may seem difficult because the past is there. So, sit as if there is no past. Here and now is all there is. There is nothing that has happened in the past. The past has disappeared… It has been erased.

   If there is no future, there is nothing to do, so do nothing. If there is no past, there is nothing to think, so just be here and now.

   No past, no future. Nothing to do, nowhere to go, no targets to achieve, no past to correct.

   No urge to fulfil anything. No desire to achieve anything. No need to worry about anything.

7. Experience the peace and relaxation. There is no topic for the mind to ruminate upon.

8. If the mind brings on a wish, or a thought, if it reminds you of something, tell the mind that there is no future now; the past has disappeared in the expanse of now.

9. This is the only moment of truth, where you are truly alive. Meditate on this emptiness. You are free… You are freedom.

10. There are no contents around. If something is sensed, neglect it. Any voice from outside, any external sensation – just ignore them.

11. Rest in this experience of emptiness till the times goes off. Then slowly open your eyes.

In situations, where we get stressed in the present, let's understand how to deal with them in the next chapter.

Action plan

- Identify impending situations in your life, which are more than a month away. Apply the mantra, "Bother then, when then becomes now."

16
Learn by Hindsight to Relax with Foresight

Jay's uncle, who was staying abroad, passed away due to heart failure. But the news about his demise never reached Jay. Though they were not regularly connected, Jay was very fond of his uncle.

Jay led his usual life, unaware of his uncle's demise. After a few months, Jay met with a motor accident and passed away.

Consider another case of Arun who received a call in the middle of the night from his friend that his batchmate Ritesh had suffered a heart failure and passed away. Now Arun started worrying, "Poor Ritesh! He was doing so well in his career. These days anything can happen to anyone. Life is so unpredictable. I fall short of breath when I climb the stairs. Hope I am not suffering a heart ailment."

Incidents being the same with Jay's uncle and Ritesh, there is a striking contrast in what happened with Jay and Arun.

Isn't it a wonder that Jay never suffered the grief of his uncle's death during his life? As he never came to know about it, he never had any thoughts about it. On the contrary, Arun was mortified and filled with all kinds of fearful thoughts.

So, what's the point?

This shows that the real culprits of our suffering are the thoughts that arise within us in response to incidents. It is our thoughts that create sorrow, anxiety, fear and worry. If it were not for the thoughts, we would dwell in our original state of joy and peace.

Life throws up situations that can shake up our mind. We get flooded with a barrage of negative thoughts during such situations. We worry that such incidents should not happen with us. We begin to fear and feel insecure. As a result, we feel drained of energy.

At such junctures, we need to consciously ask ourselves: "How was the state of my mind just before this incident? And more importantly, how will I look at it a few years from now? What will the state of my mind be after a few years with regards to this incident?"

Arun should ask himself, "How was I feeling just before I received the call? I was relaxed. What happened suddenly? Nothing really happened to me. Then why has the state of my mind changed? Can I regain the same composure as it was before these worrisome thoughts began?"

It is natural that bad news, when heard afresh, can have a deep impact on our mind. But with the passage of time, it diffuses and loses its intensity. We even forget about it completely in due course. We no longer feel sad about it after we have forgotten about it.

Consider the difficult times that you have been through a few years ago. How do you perceive them now? Don't you cherish them that they were worthwhile? But did you honor them when you were in the midst of all that was happening?

There are so many incidents that occur in our lives that we unduly fret and fume about. At such times, we see no way out. But after a few months or years, we would see that we are free from the feelings that had gripped us then.

Most people would agree that they had unnecessarily exaggerated the value of what was happening and worried too much. Some people even laugh at the way they were worrying unnecessarily in the past and remember those times with pride, as to how they overcame their challenges and emerged successful.

Students tend to be stressed and worried about their studies preparing for their exams. They find it painful to go through those tough times when they have to struggle and work hard for long hours. But after a few years, when they have progressed in their journey of life and settled down in their careers, they remember their times spent at school and university with a sense of nostalgia and exclaim, "Those were the wonderful years that can never come back… the best years of my life!"

You would have heard of many rags-to-riches stories – the lives of famous industrialists and motivational speakers, film stars and celebrities. Their candid interviews bear testimony to the tough times that they had to go through during their formative years in poverty, sleeping on pavements, going hungry. Having gone through such difficult times, when they reach the zenith of success, they feel proud when they remember their past – that they didn't break down during those testing times, but emerged stronger.

Problems are the furnace in which our characters get tempered to shine like gold. Tiding through difficulties only makes us stronger, allowing us to unleash our latent potential, leading to growth.

We need to remind ourselves, "This has only come to push me further, to make me grow. It has come to raise me to new heights of success."

By virtue of hindsight, we all can look back at our journeys till now and point at those difficult times that contributed to our present success. But when we were actually going through those testing situations, we lacked this perspective that we carry today. Wouldn't it be great if we could perceive problems and difficult times this way when we are in the midst of it?

Can't we look at what we are going through now, as we would when we look back at it in the future? We need to learn from hindsight to relax with this foresight!

There are trivial incidents that happen in our daily life – the teacup falls and breaks; the bread gets burnt in the toaster; we forget the umbrella and get drenched in the rain.

In such situations, we can ask ourselves, "How will I look at the breaking of the teacup after some years? How bad will I feel about the burnt bread after a few months? How angry will I feel about my drenched clothes next month? Will I still fret and be flustered then?" We will surely get "No" for an answer!

We may be fretting today if we cannot afford a car; we have to travel by train and walk in the rain. But when we own a car and drive in the rain a few years from now, we will exclaim, "Those were the days! We used to walk in this rain." Then the memories of getting wet in the rain will give you joy, not sorrow.

Whatever we will think and say in the distant future, why not say it today! What is stopping us? We need to inculcate the habit of saying it today.

When engulfed by difficulties, question yourself. Return to your original state before the trouble started brewing in your mind. The temporary stress and worry will dissolve by itself. You will regain your state of happiness and poise.

In the next chapter, we will look at how we can deal with our complaints and resentful thoughts about the world that pull us away from the joy of the present.

Action plan

- Contemplate on how you will look at the problems you are facing now after few years from now?
- Look at the troublesome incidents in your present with the perspective gained in this chapter.

17

No One to be Blamed

Rajan was strolling outside his office with his colleague Varun during lunch break. All of a sudden, a bird let loose above Rajan, depositing a messy smear of droppings on his head. Rajan was embarrassed. Varun laughed, "It's good that it was just a bird. What if cows were to fly in the sky?"

Jokes apart, when birds smear their droppings on us, we consider it as a natural happening, as if it is a parcel given to us by nature. In fact, in Indian and Turkish traditions, it is believed to be a good omen to receive bird droppings! But sometimes, the parcel can take the shape of stones or whatever birds carry during their flight! But we just accept it and move ahead in life.

However, when someone shouts at us, we fail to consider it as the parcel given by nature. Instead, we blame and shout back at them.

A manager leaves for his office in the morning. On the way, a dog happens to bite him. Furious, he reaches his office and shouts at his subordinate over a petty issue. The subordinate becomes upset over the unnecessary rebuke and vents his anger at the office boy, asking him why he hasn't brought him his cup of tea yet. The office boy gets irritated and shouts at the tea vendor asking him to hurry up. The tea vendor thrusts the tray into his hands, turns to his son playing around his legs and hits him for interfering with his work. The son gets angry and flings a stone at the same dog that bit the manager. Now the dog sets off in search of a new person to bite.

It is a law of nature that anything you shoot at the world, boomerangs on you; what goes around, comes around.

When someone shouts at us, we fail to understand that it's actually our parcel that nature is returning to us through him. He is not to be blamed. He is just an agent delivering our parcel.

The parcel can be praise or blame, fame or shame. If we blame the delivery agent for the parcel, we are again shooting a new arrow and nature will again return it to us through someone. Thus, the game of parcels will continue forever. It's time to take pause and consider how long we want to continue this game or whether we want to stop it now.

Yes, you read it right! You can stop this game. Let's understand how to stop this with an example.

> A game is going on between 2 opponents, A and B.
>
> In Scene 1, A shoots at B, B in turn shoots at A. This goes on for some time.
>
> In Scene 2, A shoots at B, B also shoots back at A. Then A stops shooting back at B, but B continues to shoot at A.
>
> In Scene 3, both A and B have stopped shooting at each other.

We can understand the concept of parcels from this example. The arrows of negative thoughts that we have shot at others, boomerang on us. Nature delivers them through someone or the other. Nature's preferred delivery agents are the people who are close to us. They can be our parents, siblings, spouse, children, boss, colleagues, to name a few.

Ayesha always wonders why all people are nice to her except for those at her home and office. If only those people are changed, life would be so beautiful.

What Ayesha doesn't understand is that she cannot blame these people. They are just delivering her own parcels from nature. *She* has created those parcels, not they. So instead of reacting to them, she needs to mentally seek forgiveness from them and gracefully accept all her parcels. For seeking forgiveness, she can perform the following prayer:

Dear <Name of the person>

Please forgive me for hurting or blaming you

knowingly or unknowingly

through my thoughts, feelings, words or actions.

I also forgive you.

As it happens in Scene 1 in the above example, she will get back her parcels so long as she keeps shooting at them. The moment she stops shooting, as it happens in Scene 2, she will just receive the parcels for the old arrows that she had shot earlier. Then, as it happens in Scene 3, a time comes when she won't receive any more parcels.

Seeking forgiveness does not mean that we are inferior or guilty. It only implies that we are prepared to take up the responsibility of mending what has gone wrong in our world. It requires courage and fortitude to embrace forgiveness. By forgiving or seeking forgiveness, we are not doing a favor on anyone else, but ensuring our own clarity and growth.

When you practice forgiveness, you become aware of your feelings in every situation. Instead of sowing seeds of negativity, you consciously sow seeds of faith and goodwill. Nature will then shoot back these arrows of goodwill at you.

Awareness is the key to ensure that you do not sow any negative seeds. If you sow any seeds unconsciously, instantly erase them through the practice of forgiveness. This way, you can lead an awakened life.

People around you are Co-creators of your Life

> Suppose a little child wants to play cricket, but has no one to play with. He insists that his father should play with him. The father is not very interested, but loves his child and doesn't want to dishearten him. So, he agrees.
>
> The child prefers to bat and improve his game, so that he can be selected for his school team. What does the father do? Of course, he will bowl, so that his darling child can practice batting! Not that he likes to bowl, but he would still do it out of love for his child.
>
> Now, the father would love to see his child improve his game and be selected for higher league matches. So what does he do? He bowls bouncers and googlies (disguised spinning balls) at his child. The child feels let down when he is unable to face the ball effectively and protests that his father is unfair. He even complains that his father does not love him, and hence is making batting difficult for him.
>
> The father then explains to his child lovingly that he is raising the difficulty level of the game, only to let his son become an expert at the game and hit the ball out of the ground with confidence, without being flustered by googlies or bouncers. He teaches his son to read the bowling carefully so that he can hit the bouncers and googlies for sixes and fours.
>
> When the child learns the art of getting on top of the bowling and batting with poise and confidence, he feels grateful for his father's contribution to his success.

In the game of cricket, you need someone to bowl at you so that you can bat. Without bowlers, you can never get to bat and you won't be able to mature into an ace batsman.

This metaphorical game of cricket between the father and the child resembles the game of life. The father here represents your relationships – your family, friends, neighbors, colleagues, managers, subordinates, your local civic services and also the government! All these people, who play a variety of roles in your daily life, avail you the opportunity to mature and develop vital qualities like patience, uncompromising love, playfulness, consistency, resilience, creativity, steadfastness, to name a few. It is only when you develop these higher qualities that you truly grow and mature and bring about a transformation within and around you.

When someone helps you in a way that's obvious, you feel that they wish you well. However, when someone puts you down, or constrains your progress, or poses problems in your career, you feel they are being unfair by bowling real-life bouncers and googlies at you.

Consider people around you as partners, as contributors, as co-creators in the journey of your life. Those who arouse contempt within you, those who trigger negative thoughts within you, actually deserve your understanding. They may be playing a negative role in your life, only because they are co-creators, contributing to your growth.

As we have discussed earlier in the chapter "Reflect on Yourself", choose to see the negativity that the other person provokes within you as a mirror and recognize the opportunity for self-introspection. The other person is contributing to co-create positive qualities within you.

When you catch yourself blaming or having resentful thoughts about people, remember that the essence of your thoughts are seeds that shape your life. Ask yourself whether that is really the experience that you want to create.

Let's understand how we can look at calamities in our life happily in the next chapter.

Action plan

- At night before you sleep, seek forgiveness from all those people whom you have hurt knowingly or unknowingly. Forgive those who hurt you.

- Contemplate on what kind of role the people nearby are playing in your life and the opportunity to develop qualities.

18
Hold Onto Your Happy Hat

When we are alert, we can break the negative stream of thoughts and shift to a different stream. However, sometimes we get into such situations where our thoughts overpower us. They gain so much momentum that despite our will, we are unable to stop them. At such times, the Happy Hat Habit comes to our rescue.

> The owner of a circus had pitched his circus tent on the outskirts of the city. Just a day before the show, there came a violent storm that blew away the tent.
>
> The circus owner was a veteran who had seen the rough of life. While the members of the troupe were running helter-skelter, worrying how they will put up the show, the trapeze artist caught sight of the owner walking around with an enigmatic smile.
>
> Seeing his smile of assurance, the trapeze artist told the others, "I have seen our boss smile. I don't think we need to be worried. Let's go and talk to him." They approached him, asking what they should be doing next.
>
> Before instructing them on how to salvage the weathered tent, he gave them a very important message: "The tent may have blown away, but hold onto your happy hat, lest you lose that too... the show is far from over!"

Negative situations that come in life are akin to the storm. They could be either a heavy loss in business, the sudden demise of a close one, failure in exams, being fired from a job, to name a few. They can blow away your roof; everything can get into disarray. You may lose direction in life. Life may seem hopeless. You may feel as if all the miseries of the world have befallen you. Despite this, hold your happy hat tight.

You cannot control the situation. The disaster has happened. It could be the result of your negative thoughts in the past, or nature's wondrous way of bringing you growth that you could never have thought of. If you still think negatively about why the incident happened and blame the situation or people, you are sowing negative seeds. They will bear negative fruit. Thus, this cycle will go on.

But when you retain your happy hat, you remain happy in the midst of such situations. You stop the momentum of negative thoughts and their after-effect. Your positive state helps neutralize the worsening effect of the situation. You recognize the need of the hour and sow positive seeds with awareness for a bright future. These positive thoughts gain momentum and attract the next progressive scene in your life. Soon, you find yourself out of the situation.

When calamities come, they may seem to ravage our surroundings, but the least we can do in these circumstances is to hold onto our happy hat. No matter what problems arise in your life, ask yourself, "Has my happy hat blown off?" Catch hold of it. If your happy hat has gone, then the reconstruction of your roof becomes more difficult. If you keep your happy hat intact, you can construct a concrete roof. The old roof blew away only because the new roof had to come!

When shake-ups happen in your life, remember that there is a replacement going on, some shuffling is going on. New scenes are being brought into your life. As we are not aware of what's going to happen next, we try to resist the situation. However, if we remain happy amidst all situations of our life, we help the next scene to unfold. Who knows, the next scene could be better than the previous one, just like the concrete roof for the circus.

Thus, for some problems where you can't help the situation, just retain your happy hat. You may find it difficult to be happy in such perilous and sorrowful situations. In order to retain your happy hat, you may either watch a comedy show, or go on a nature trail, or listen to some music that delights you. Start gathering your hat of happiness and count your blessings.

Record the feelings of gratitude, because we often forget the good things that have happened in our lives when we get burdened with our problems. However, we do not fail to dwell on the negative things that occur in our life.

Being in gratitude loosens the grip of negative feelings. Our focus shifts from scarcity to abundance. Abundance then begins to show up in our life. When we abide in the state of joy, regardless of circumstances, we become a magnet that attracts the most suitable solutions to our problems. When you hold onto the happy feeling especially during sorrowful situations, you transmit happy vibrations to nature. Due to this, nature brings you more experiences of happiness. When you send out vibrations of sorrow, nature creates similar situations where you experience more of sorrow.

Gratitude has immense power. If you are grateful about everything in life, you automatically and constantly focus on the best. You remain in harmony with whatever is, which makes you receptive to the unfolding of your highest possibilities. You break through all limitations in your thinking and invoke the divine qualities within you. You automatically move away from doubts, worries and the feeling of scarcity.

We have seen the importance of the habit of holding onto your happy hat. In the next chapter, we will look at the need to drop the habit of copycat.

Action plan

- Prepare a Gratitude diary and start writing down things that you can be grateful for. It may be the most trivial thing like the bright blue morning sky or your neighbor's smile. Keep adding to it on a daily basis. Read it when you tend to feel dejected and bring back the rich memories into your awareness.

19

Drop The Copycat Habit

Sneha was going on her morning walk when she saw her neighbor Pratibha near the entrance gate of the park. She smiled at her, but Pratibha was lost in her own thoughts. She just ignored Sneha. Sneha felt put down by Pratibha's callous response, or rather the lack of any response, "She just ignored me. Next time I will also ignore her. I won't smile at her."

The next day Pratibha remembered what had happened the previous morning only when she saw Sneha. She felt, "Oh… perhaps I hadn't responded to Sneha. I should have spoken to her even though I was lost in my own problems." It was Pratibha's turn to smile and she wished Sneha. But Sneha deliberately ignored her and walked the other way.

Pratibha was surprised at Sneha's behavior, "Oh! Yesterday she smiled at me. Today she just ignored me. She changes her colors every day like a chameleon. Henceforth, I too won't smile at her."

You can see how Sneha and Pratibha have copied each other's responses. This can be called the copycat habit. This happens because of mirror neurons in our brain. Mirror neurons are a type of brain cells that fire either when we do a particular action, or when we simply watch someone else performing an action.

> When you watch your favorite actor whom you idolize, you may have noticed that you somewhat imitate the actor unknowingly after walking out of the cinema. Your body language may momentarily change to mirror your idol's behavior, perhaps in the subtlest ways.

This happens because your mirror neurons get activated while you watch the movie. They function on the belief that you are actually performing the actor's role. For the same reason, when you read some news about a road accident, you may believe the same could happen to you too. You may feel terrified when you watch a horror movie. When you listen to a motivational speaker, or read a biography, you may feel inspired.

Mirror neurons constantly fire and try to imitate whatever they see, hear or feel. They help in understanding the actions and intentions of other people, and in learning new skills through imitation. The mirror neuron system plays a key role in your ability to empathize, socialize, and communicate your emotions. How strongly your mirror neurons' system gets activated determines how empathetic you feel.

Mirror neurons play a vital role in human learning experience. When we see a dance choreographer move, we replicate his moves. Like a mirror, we look at what he is doing, replicate the same steps and learn. We are able to do this because of these neurons, which have been given so that they are used in a positive way.

We can put our mirror neurons to use in developing our virtues by observing others. Just by observing others' virtues, reading motivational biographies, watching inspiring movies where these qualities are demonstrated, we plant positive seeds for our own future. That is the true purpose of mirror neurons.

However, when we use them for blindly copying others' responses, we are not putting them to use for the purpose they were intended. It would then be like monkeys; copying whatever we see.

For instance, if someone smiles at us, we will smile back at them. If they don't smile at us, we too don't smile. Our smile becomes an expensive commodity! We do not know the circumstances surrounding that person when they did not return our smile. The next day, the person comes all set to smile at us and we coldly turn and walk away, just as Sneha did in the earlier example. Now we have ensured that we are monkeying. Seeing our behavior, the other person also decides not to smile. Now both are monkeying!

Just because of the copycat habit, we depend upon others to make us happy. If they don't behave as per our desire, we sulk within. We change our behavior. We lower our awareness by imitating them. We deviate from our original happy nature. Hence, we need to break this harmful copycat habit.

Suppose that you are travelling on a train and your co-passenger is reading a newspaper. What do you do? Do you also read the newspaper? He is reading a newspaper, so must I. The co-passenger twitches his ears every now and then; would you also start doing that just because he is doing it? If he sits down on the floor just below his seat; would you imitate him and sit on the floor? Why wouldn't you? You do not want to copy that. However, when the other person is not talking to you, you copy that. How does this happen unknown to you?

We need to remind ourselves – those ancestral, monkey like learnings are over – this is the new age. Now we are human. We need to remind ourselves, because we should unlock the potential that comes from being human. Regardless of the other's behavior, we should behave according to our original happy nature. When we connect with our originality, our happiness, love and caring nature will reflect in our behavior unconditionally.

If the other person doesn't wish you "Good morning" and you too do not feel like wishing him back due to the copycat habit, take a pause. Ask yourself, "Why do I need to copy others?" Go ahead and wish the other person, regardless. You can do this because your morning is good. If he doesn't, he is only saying that his morning is perhaps not as good!

We can do it because we are not monkeys; we are human. Even if the other person does not strike a conversation with you, you must seize the initiative. You should do it for yourself. You can behave originally if your awareness has risen.

Instead of just expecting others to act or say something, we must take the first step and be firm on it. We need to be decisive. We shouldn't refrain from doing the correct thing by citing lame excuses. We need not copy others. There are bigger things to do… so many things are waiting to happen in our lives. Original creations and initiatives can manifest when we drop the copycat habit.

As we drop the copycat habit, our mind stops troubling us. We begin to shape our future by being aware in the present, instead of copying from our past. In the next chapter, we will discuss how we can carve our future by being in the present.

Action plan

- In daily life situations, observe where you respond by the copycat habit. Consciously decide how you can respond originally and act accordingly.

20

Consciously Create Your Future

Life is a series of incidents. From morning till night, we go through a series of incidents. Our mind considers some incidents as problems and resists them. At the same time, it considers certain other incidents as opportunities and favors them. We experience pain with problems and pleasure with opportunities.

When we react negatively to problems, we sow the seeds of more problems in our future. When we positively respond to opportunities, we pave the way for our growth. Thus, the way we choose to consider an incident as a problem or an opportunity decides whether we beget happiness or sorrow in the future.

Based on the past conditioning of our mind, if we perceive the incident as a problem, we tend to resist it, plant the seeds of negative feelings, thereby bringing complications in our life. However, if we consider the incident as a stepping stone to awaken us towards growth and fulfillment, we welcome it as an opportunity. If we change our perspective of looking at problems, they help us learn our lessons of life. They point at those areas of our life where we lack awareness and understanding.

If your life lesson is to learn patience and courage then you will experience incidents that will help you develop patience, that will bring out the courage that lies latent within you. People will behave with you in ways that you will lose your patience. In some incidents, you may feel scared. At such junctures, if you let your old programming take over, then the vices like anger, boredom, comparison, ego, fear, hatred, ill-will, jealousy will play out through you. The other person will look for opportunities to settle the score with you and retort in a similar manner. Thus, this vicious cycle of action and reaction will go on without an end.

In order to break free from this mechanical way of living, we need to give a creative response by being aware in the present. We need to change the way we respond to incidents. We will follow a different sequence of steps in our response to any incident as follows:

- Consider every **incident** as an **opportunity** for growth.

- Ask yourself, "Can I accept it?" **Accept** the incident or people exactly as they are.

- This enables you to make a new start. Instead of giving a copycat response, you **give a new happy response,** by watching the scene from the standpoint of pure awareness.

- As you give a new happy response, it sows healthy seeds for your future. Thus, you **create your future by sowing seeds in the present.** You don't let the past create your future.

In the example cited in the previous chapter, even if Pratibha doesn't pay heed to Sneha, Sneha will wish her the next day. Thus, Sneha's response is independent of how Pratibha behaves. She sows new positive seeds for her future by being aware of her response in the present.

Thus, you need to change the **effect** of every incident into an **opportunity**, practice **acceptance**, give a **happy response** and **sow the seeds for the future by being vigilant in the present.**

Faith Fair Diary

In order to sow seeds of faith, reflect on what you really want in your life and consciously sow those seeds. At this juncture, a Faith Fair Diary can come handy to you.

The Faith Fair Diary is a paper notebook or a journaling tool on your computer or mobile. It helps you gain clarity about what you really want in life and why. It is like your personal companion that will accompany you every day and every moment, reminding you about your life choices, your key decisions and the principles that you have chosen to live by, and why.

The reason it is called a "Faith" Fair Diary is because you write and read with full faith that nature will bring you whatever you have scripted in it.

Write down the goal of your life and precisely explain how you wish to lead your life and why. The more lofty or the more noble goal you have, the more you will need to maintain your Faith Fair Diary. It helps maintain sharp focus on the goal without being influenced by negative circumstances.

Ensure that you maintain a single Faith Fair Diary. Write down only what you want in life; not what you don't want. For example, instead of writing "I don't want to fall sick," write "I want to enjoy good health."

Clearly state why you want to achieve your goals by adding "so that" in your sentences. This will make it easier for you to achieve them. Write it in the present tense even though it is a future goal. The idea is to ingrain in your subconscious that it has already happened or is happening. Here are a few examples.

- I am becoming wealthier with every passing day so that I am not only financially stable, but also able to help others in need.

- I have attained complete health so that I can take giant strides towards success in my chosen field.

- I complete all my tasks smoothly so that I am enjoying a healthy balance between my personal and professional life, thus becoming more peaceful, happy and satisfied.

- I have committed and loyal colleagues in my office so that we create better products and services in our field of work which spreads happiness and wellbeing in the world.

- I have a good salary, and am growing at my workplace with the cooperation of my colleagues so that I fulfil all my responsibilities effectively and assist in the progress of the organization.

- I live in a world where there is an abundance of everything for everyone to co-exist peacefully, so that everyone experiences love and bliss.

Before writing your wants in your Faith Fair Diary, you may write them in a rough notebook. This gives you the flexibility to refine what you've written on the go. Once you are sure about it, you can write them in your Faith Fair Diary with the faith that nature will manifest it in your life.

Once you write your Faith Fair Diary, read it three to four times a week with full faith with a feeling of fulfillment. Reading it will raise your awareness and also activate the power of thought. Soon, the imagined state will become your reality.

When you practice this with persistence, before you realize it, you will see that your future has begun to change for the better. Your relations with those around you will begin to be harmonious, your life will begin to abound in health and prosperity. You will witness new wondrous vistas unfolding in each area of your life. You will be able to unleash your potential.

Your body-mind will get updated and upgraded to become the best aircraft for who-you-truly-are! The caterpillar will be transformed into a beautiful butterfly that takes flight.

Action plan

- Identify the incidents in your daily life where you give copycat reactions based on habits from the past. Review your day for such reactions. Change them based on the steps outlined above.

- Create a Faith Fair Diary and write down what you want in your life. Categorize your wants into sections like Physical, Social, Financial, Professional, Spiritual etc.

You can send your opinion or feedback on this book to:
Tej Gyan Foundation, P.O. Box 25, Pimpri Colony, Pimpri, Pune – 411017, Maharashtra, INDIA
Email: englishbooks@tejgyan.org

Write for Us

We welcome writers, translators and editors to join our team. If you would like to volunteer, please email us at: englishbooks@tejgyan.org or call : +91 90110 10963

About Sirshree

Sirshree's spiritual quest, which began during his childhood, led him on a journey through various schools of thought and prevalent meditation practices. His overpowering desire to attain the Truth made him relinquish his teaching profession. After a long period of contemplation on the truth of life, his spiritual quest culminated in the attainment of the ultimate truth. Since then, over the last two decades, he has dedicated his life toward elevating mass consciousness and making spiritual pursuit simple and accessible to all.

Sirshree espouses, "**All paths that lead to the truth begin differently, but culminate at the same point – understanding. Understanding is complete in itself. Listening to this understanding is enough to attain the truth.**"

Sirshree has delivered more than 3000 discourses that throw light on this understanding, simplify various aspects of life and unravel missing links in spirituality. He delivers the understanding in casual contemporary language by weaving profound aspects into analogies, parables and humor that provoke one to contemplate.

To make it possible for people from all walks of life to directly experience this understanding, Sirshree has designed the *Maha Aasmani Param Gyan Shivir* – a retreat designed as a comprehensive system for imparting wisdom. This system for wisdom, which has been accredited with ISO 9001:2015 certification, has inspired thousands of seekers from all walks of life to progress on their journey of the Truth. This system makes the wisdom accessible to every human being, regardless of religion, caste, social strata, country or belief system.

Sirshree is the founder of Tej Gyan Foundation, a no-profit organization committed to raising mass consciousness with branches in India, the United States, Europe and Asia-Pacific. Sirshree's retreats have transformed the lives of thousands and his teachings have inspired various social initiatives for raising global consciousness.

His published work includes more than 100 books, some of which have been translated in more than 10 languages and published by leading publishers. Sirshree's books provide profound and practical reading on existential subjects like emotional maturity, harmony in relationships, developing self-belief, overcoming stress and anxiety, and dealing with the question of life-beyond-death, to name a few. His literature on core spirituality expounds the deeper meaning of self-realization and self-stabilization, unravelling missing links in the understanding of karma, wisdom, devotion, meditation and consciousness.

Various luminaries and celebrities like His Holiness the Dalai Lama, publishers Mr. Reid Tracy, Ms. Tami Simon and Yoga Master Dr. B. K. S. Iyengar have released Sirshree's books and lauded his work. "The Source" book series, authored by Sirshree, has sold over 10 million copies in 5 years. His book, "The Warrior's Mirror", published by Penguin, was featured in the Limca Book of Records for being released on the same day in 11 languages.

Tejgyan... The Road Ahead
What is Tejgyan?

Tejgyan is the wisdom of the existential truth, which is beyond duality. "Gyan" is a term commonly used for "knowledge". Tejgyan is the wisdom beyond knowledge and ignorance. It is understanding that arises from direct experience of the final truth. It is what sets us free from the limitations of the mind and opens us to our highest potential.

In today's world, there are people who feel disharmony and are desperately trying to achieve balance in an unpredictable life. Tejgyan helps them in harmonizing with their true nature, the Self, thereby restoring balance in all aspects of their lives.

And then, there are those who are successful, but feel a sense of emptiness within. Tejgyan provides them fulfilment and helps them to embark on a journey towards self-realization. There are others who feel lost and are seeking the meaning of life. Tejgyan helps them to realize the true purpose of human life.

All this is possible with Tejgyan due to a very simple reason. The experience of the ultimate truth (God or Pure consciousness) is always available. The direct experience of this truth is possible provided the right method is known. Tejgyan is that method, that understanding.

The understanding of Tejgyan makes it possible to lead a life of freedom from fear, worry, anger and stress. It helps in attaining physical vitality, emotional strength and stability, harmony in relationships, financial freedom and spiritual progress.

At Tej Gyan Foundation, Sirshree imparts this understanding through a System for Wisdom – a series of retreats that guides participants step by step towards realizing the true Self, being established in the experience of self-realization, and expressing its qualities. This system for wisdom has been accredited with the ISO 9001:2015 certification.

Maha Aasmani Param Gyan Shivir

"**Maha Aasmani Param Gyan Shivir**" is the flagship Self-realization retreat offered by Tej Gyan Foundation. The retreat is conducted in Hindi. The teachings of the retreat are non-denominational (secular).

This residential retreat is held for 3 to 5 days at the foundation's MaNaN Ashram amidst the glory of the mountains and the pristine beauty of nature. The Ashram is located at the outskirts of the city of Pune in India, and is well connected by air, road and rail. The retreat is also held at other centres of Tej Gyan Foundation across the world.

You can participate in this retreat to attain ageless wisdom through a unique System for Wisdom so that you can:

1. Discover "Who am I" through direct experience.
2. Learn to abide in pure consciousness while functioning in the world, allowing the qualities of consciousness like peace, love, joy, compassion, abundance and creativity to manifest.
3. Acquire simple tools to use in everyday life, which help quiet the chattering mind.
4. Get practical techniques to be in the present and connect to the source of all answers within (the inner guru).
5. Discover missing links in the practices of Meditation (*Dhyana*), Action (*Karma*), Wisdom (*Gyana*) and Devotion (*Bhakti*).
6. Understand the nature of your body-mind mechanism to attain freedom form its tendencies.
7. Learn practical methods to shift from mind-centered living to consciousness-centered living.

A Mini-retreat is also conducted, especially for teenagers (14 to 16 years of age) during summer and winter vacations.

To register for retreats, visit www.tejgyan.org,
contact (+91) 9921008060, or email mail@tejgyan.com

About Tej Gyan Foundation

Tej Gyan Foundation (TGF) was established with the mission of creating a highly evolved society through all-round development of every individual that transforms all the facets of their lives. It is a non-profit organization, founded on the teachings of Sirshree.

The Foundation has received the ISO certification (ISO 9001:2015) for its system of imparting wisdom. It has centres all across India as well as in other countries. The motto of Tej Gyan Foundation is 'Happy Thoughts'.

At the core of the philosophy of Tejgyan is the Power of Acceptance. Acceptance has profound meaning and is at the core of our Being. It is Acceptance that brings forth true love, joy and peace.

Symbol of Acceptance

The Symbol of Acceptance – shown above – is a representation of this truth. The symbol represents brackets. Whatever occurs in life falls within these brackets that signify acceptance of whatever *is*. Hence, this symbol forms the centerpiece of the Foundation's MaNaN Ashram.

The Foundation is creating a highly evolved society through:
- Tejgyan Programs (Retreats, YouTube Webcasts)
- Tejgyan Books and Apps
- Tejgyan Projects (Value education, Women empowerment, Peace initiatives)

The Foundation undertakes projects to elevate the level of consciousness among students, youth, women, senior citizens, teachers, doctors, leaders, professionals, corporate and Government organizations, police force, prisoners etc.

Now you can register online for
the following retreats

Maha Aasmani Param Gyan Shivir
(5 Days Residential Retreat in Hindi)

Mini Maha Aasmani Shivir
3 Days (Residential) Retreat for Teens

🔍 www.tejgyan.org

Books can be delivered at your doorstep by registered post or courier. You can request the same through postal money order or pay by VPP. Please send the money order to either of the following two addresses:

WOW Publishings Pvt. Ltd.

1. Registered Office: E-4, Vaibhav Nagar, Near Tapovan Mandir, Pimpri, Pune - 411017.

2. Post Box No. 36, Pimpri Colony Post Office, Pimpri, Pune - 411017

Phone No: (+91) 9011013210 / 9146285129

You can also order your copy at the online store:
www.gethappythoughts.org

*Free Shipping plus 10% Discount on purchases above Rs. 500/-

For further details contact:
Tejgyan Global Foundation
Registered Office:

Happy Thoughts Building, Vikrant Complex, Near Tapovan Mandir, Pimpri, Pune 411017, Maharashtra, India.
Contact No: 020-27411240, 27412576
Email: mail@tejgyan.com
MaNaN Ashram:

Survey No. 43, Sanas Nagar, Nandoshi gaon, Kirkatwadi Phata, Sinhagad Road, Tal. Haveli, Dist. Pune 411024, Maharashtra, India.
Contact No: 992100 8060.

Hyderabad: 9885558100, **Bangalore:** 9880412588,
Delhi : 9891059875, **Nashik:** 9326967980, **Mumbai:** 9373440985

For accessing our unique 'System for Wisdom' from self-help to self-realization, please follow us on:

	Website Online Shopping/ Blog	www.tejgyan.org www.gethappythoughts.org
	Video Channel	www.youtube.com/tejgyan For Q&A videos: http://goo.gl/YA81DQ
	Social networking	www.facebook.com/tejgyan
	Social networking	www.twitter.com/sirshree
	Internet Radio	http://www.tejgyan.org/ internetradio.aspx

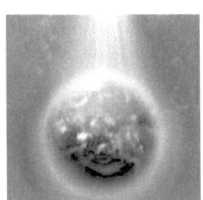

Pray for World Peace along with thousands of others every day at 09:09am and 09:09pm

Divine Light of Love, Bliss and Peace is Showering;
The Golden Light of Higher Consciousness is Rising;
All negativity on Earth is Dissolving;
Everyone is in Peace and Blissfully Shining;
O God, Gratitude for Everything!

www.ingramcontent.com/pod-product-compliance
Lightning Source LLC
LaVergne TN
LVHW040154080526
838202LV00042B/3149